A *novel of*

Of
Oceans
and
Pearls

RENEE KNIGHT

To The One,

My Heavenly Father

He healeth the broken in heart,

and bindeth up their wounds.

— King David

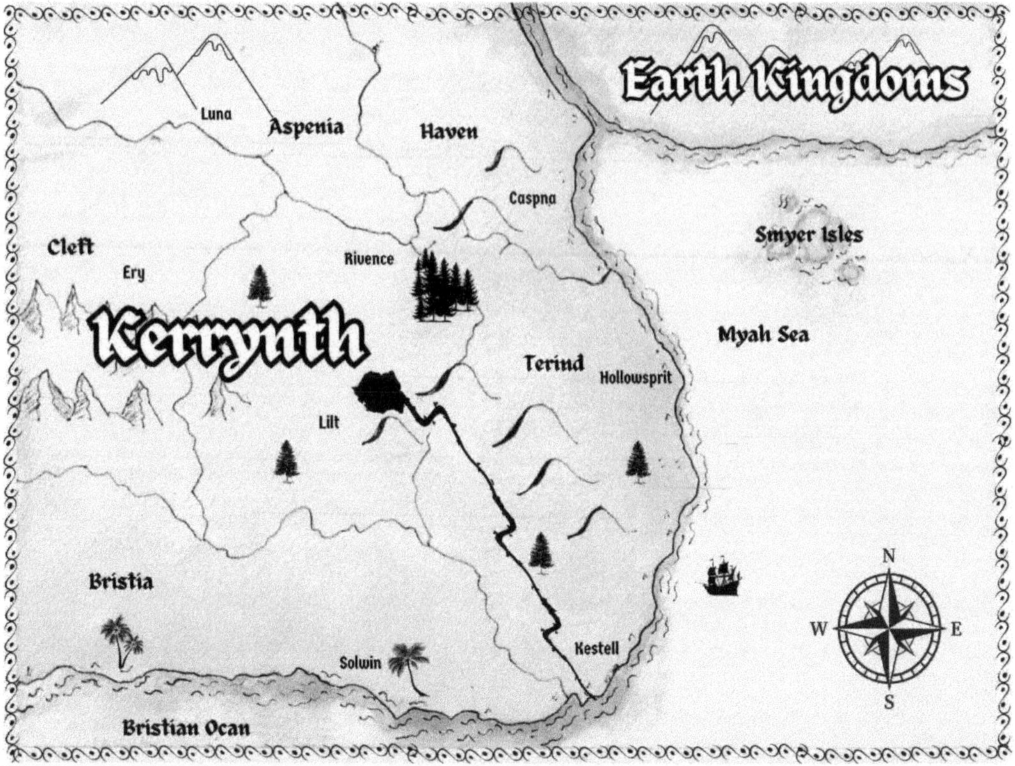
Earth Kingdoms
Luna
Aspenia
Haven
Caspna
Smyer Isles
Cleft
Ery
Rivence
Kerrynth
Myah Sea
Terind
Hollowsprit
Lilt
Bristia
N
W
E
S
Kestell
Solwin
Bristian Ocan

CHAPTER ONE

Present

Joran sniffed and glanced around. The tavern was full, but no one noticed him in the shadowy corner. Good. Rivence, home of his family's summer castle, wasn't a huge town, and he had been to all of its taverns this summer, so he had to be careful. Even though his guards were still at the castle, he knew the city guard might also have been alerted to keep an eye out for him, and he didn't need the news of who he was spreading.

In here, he wasn't a prince. He was just a miserable young man hoping the warmth of liquor and noise of the reveling would fill his insides enough to push away the turmoil. He grit his teeth together because so far it wasn't working. There was a game of cards going on across the room. He strode toward the group who was settled around two joined tables. They took one look at his smooth, young face and sneered.

"What's this? A dandy wants to try his hand with us?" The man opposite Joran drawled. His beard was thick and unruly, and he was too large for the small chair.

Joran was used to people dismissing him because of his fine clothes and smooth style. He didn't have a rough look to make them believe he was a threat. That was a good thing. It meant they often let down their guards around him. He was also noticeably younger than the men around the table. He didn't mind being the center of attention though, not as long as he wasn't recognized and dragged back to the castle.

He sat down hard, his eyes fixed on the heavy man who appeared to be the leader. He added some coins to the pile on the table and a man reluctantly dealt him cards.

He loved the feel of the worn cards in his grasp. It centered him. He fanned them out, already pleased with his hand. A few rounds around the table and he was ready to collect his winnings. Someone spat.

He began to gather the coins, but an iron grip closed around his wrist. "Not so fast, *gentleman*. Let's raise the stakes." The big man's eyes fell to Joran's hand. The gold band around his pinky finger shone in the light from the hanging lamp above them. "Here, bet this," he challenged, trying to slide the ring off. "This is fine gold."

Joran's throat went dry. "No! I mean, no. I have something better." He reached into his pocket and withdrew a small pouch. The big man looked at it skeptically, but another man gasped.

He grinned, retrieving his wrist from the man's hold. "Pure jacin, how about that?" Joran asked, opening the pouch to reveal the gray powder inside.

A lowered voice warned, "That's illegal. Best not to show it."

Joran tossed it to the middle of the table. "And yet we're all playing for it, so who is going to tell?"

Two men dropped out, unwilling to continue with the high bet.

Chairs scratched the ground as they began a new round, and Joran let out his breath. He fisted his left hand under the table, rubbing the ring with his thumb. He had given it to Krynn two years ago, with a promise that they would never be separated. That was two days before she was killed. He would never part with it.

Joran revealed his cards with everyone else. He smirked when he saw the large man's cards. They had nearly the same hand, but Joran had a higher-ranking card. He tried not to gloat in the man's face as he reached for the pot. A meaty fist slammed into his jaw, throwing him off balance. He blinked through the sparks that filled his eyesight and swiped at the money on the center of the table, grabbing what he could.

"You cheated," his opponent bellowed drunkenly.

"Not this time," Joran retorted, ducking below another swing.

He snagged the pouch of jacin and pivoted, making a run for it.

Tables and people crowded the space between him and the door, but the heady feeling of jacin in his blood was still strong, and he felt powerful. He darted around a table, then leaped right over the next one, careening through the exit.

Cool night air had barely hit his skin when something pulled him up short. The angry man had hold of his shirt and swung him around. The others had followed and stood in a ring around Joran and the man.

"I told you I didn't cheat," Joran growled.

A fist landed in his face. The pain sank into his teeth, and he tensed against the throbbing. His nose, newly healed from his brother's punches two weeks ago, began bleeding immediately.

Other arms latched onto his, and he was pinned. He let the pain wash through him, almost enjoying the agony. The jacin helped his mind stay locked in the easy state of exhilaration, even while the pain rocked him.

The big man leaned close, small droplets of spit landing on Joran's cheek as he growled into his ear.

"No stranger comes to the Ox and Bull and ups me in front of my men. And you, some dapper boy, least of all. I'll just take these coins and smash them into your eyes, plug up your nose, and cram 'em down your throat."

Joran managed to sputter a laugh at the threat. "Terrible waste of good coin, isn't it?"

"And when you suffocate and die, I'll dig 'em out of you."

"Aren't you creative? Do you use such unique techniques on all your victims? You could make quite a name for yourself as an assassin." His voice was thick with the blood running down his throat, but the sarcasm was evident.

A slap across his face answered him.

"Shut up. You're about to die. Act like it."

Joran was about to respond with something equally ridiculous. If he kept going, maybe the drunk man really would kill him, and that ending didn't sound so bad. But there was movement behind the circle of men. He couldn't see what was happening at first, but the men suddenly parted, most scattering away into the darkness.

Castle guards. Joran rolled his eyes.

His captor released his hold.

"Move away from the Prince," a guard commanded.

The man's eyes rounded. He gaped at Joran, his hands up as he backed away.

"He – he stole – I didn't know –" he mumbled.

The guards ignored him, grabbing Joran instead. Again both of his arms were pinned. He couldn't even swipe at the blood running down his face. They pulled him along, rougher than necessary. He wasn't fighting them, and he cursed. There was no reason for them to bully him.

Except there was, he knew. They'd had to retrieve him from taverns in the middle of the night, pull him out of fights, like tonight, or drag him out of a ditch, covered in vomit, often enough in the past year.

Dunn, who had been his guard the longest, cursed too. "Spirits, boy, it's apparent you have no regard for your own life. But do you really have to do this to your father?"

Joran scoffed. His father had been incompetent for years. The Queen had used a magical crystal to control him, leaving him just a shell of a man. He had been a gentle man, but completely unaware of his sons and his kingdom. It had only been two weeks since the spell had been broken, and though the King seemed to have changed now that the power over him had disappeared, he had still been too busy to pay attention to Joran. *Just as distant as ever. Nothing has really changed,* Joran thought.

"My *father* doesn't even know when I'm gone," he bit back.

Dunn jerked his arm.

"Your father was under a spell, which has successfully been broken. He is eager to get to know you, but you don't even have the grace to face him. Don't worry, though, we have brought him up to date on your wonderfully respectful behavior."

Joran breathed through his nose, trying to clear the blood. "Perfect. It's a pity you didn't get to include my little win tonight in your report."

Rodavan, the guard on his left, snorted. "Your win, Your Highness? Excuse me, but it looked like you were outnumbered by five at least, and you had blood running down your face when we arrived."

"I'm grateful, as always," Joran spit. "Nevertheless, yes, it was a win. The big one was only angry because I won the whole pot."

Dunn shook his head. "Seriously, Joran, sober up. Your father is waiting to speak to you."

"Well, he can wait a few minutes." Joran couldn't help the remark. "After all, I've only been waiting for him my whole life."

Still, he fell into sullen silence as his men took him back to the castle, leaving only the clicking of their boots on the cobblestones to accompany their thoughts.

The refugees in the Black Forest had stormed Blackstone Castle in a revolt two weeks ago. No one had known that they were living in the forest, although there had been rumors. Just after Joran's birth, magic had been prohibited in the kingdom of his birth, Ethereal, and its protectorate, Terind. Many people with supernatural gifts had fled to other kingdoms, but apparently a group of them had disappeared in the Black Forest and carved out a life there. The Great Magister, the keeper of the source of magic and master of all of it, had hidden there too, secretly planning a revolt for years. Other magisters had ceased training in magic and simply became masters of rites and ceremonies, but the disappearance of the Great Magister had been a standing mystery until two weeks ago.

Joran had injured his own mother the night of the attack, helping stop her evil magic and allowing the Black Forest Band to capture her. Although he wasn't fighting for the same reasons they were, he was tired of his mother destroying everything in her lust for power and control. When he saw her threatening his younger brother, Golan, he'd shot her through the shoulder without hesitating. She was executed the next day.

Spirits. His mother was *dead*. Now his father finally wanted to meet with him. All of it made his gut churn, but he could really only think about one thing. The one thing that no one else even knew about, let alone cared about right now.

Krynn. Tomorrow was her birthday. He corrected himself. Tomorrow *would be* her birthday, if she was alive. He was getting older, and she wasn't, and it was the one thing he couldn't handle.

CHAPTER TWO

9 years ago

Joran kicked at the table leg in frustration, his lips set in a pout.

"Joran, look up please," Queen Lilian said tersely.

He peered up at his mother. She'd brought him along on this trip yesterday, and he had been happy then. She was going to visit some of her sisters who lived in Terind. Being the eighth of ten children meant she had more family than Joran could keep up with, and she spent at least a month every year visiting them. The prospect of no lessons for a few days had excited Joran, but traveling with his mother was much more boring than he had bargained for. Now he was in a parlor with too many flowers, waiting for his eldest aunt to appear for tea. His ten-year-old nerves could hardly handle the prospect of sitting quietly for the next hour while his mother and aunt conversed.

"There isn't anything to do here," he complained.

His mother raised her eyebrows in warning, then sighed. "Fine then. Go outside and entertain yourself this afternoon. Aunt Adeline won't notice whether you're here or not, but when we see Aunt Rhea tomorrow, I fully expect you to be on your best behavior."

Joran nodded, already on his feet. He barely heard his mother calling after him to keep quiet and not get into trouble as he bolted for the door.

The large house was ancient. Incredibly boring. The grounds however, were sprawling and graced by a shimmery pond. There were trees aplenty with low-hanging branches and lots of places to explore that looked much more exciting than afternoon tea.

***

He meandered around the pond, enjoying the splashes as frogs dove out of his way. He poked a stick down a hole, wondering if the snake was at home, but nothing came out. Now he was under a delightfully hidden tree with curtains of leaves hanging from the low branches. He grinned. Mother would be upset if she knew he was playing in these clothes, but she had been the one who had suggested going outside. He stepped into a low fork in the trunk, and let out a yelp when he caught sight of fluttering blue fabric just above him.

He looked up. A girl stood above him, her blue eyes wide.

"What are you doing?" he asked, surprised to see a girl in a tree.

She didn't answer him, just dropped her eyes shyly.

He leaned back against the trunk and folded his arms. "Do you live here?"

She glanced at him and shook her head. "My mother works for Lady Marty."

He shrugged. He didn't know a Lady Marty. "My mother is Queen Lilian of Ethereal. She came to visit her sister, Countess Adeline, so that's why I'm here."

The girl's eyes got even wider. Joran tilted his head as he studied them. His own eyes were blue, but not like hers. She had such light eyes, they looked ghostly.

"You're a prince," she breathed.

Joran grinned. "Second born prince, you're right. My name is Joran."

The girl smiled hesitantly. "I'm Krynn. My mother is Lady Marty's lady's maid. Lady Marty is good friends with Countess Adeline, so she comes here a lot, and my mother brings me when she can. I like looking for birds' nests, and the Countess has the best estate for birds. There are so many trees."

Joran didn't care about birds, but he blew out a little laugh. He would like to look for them too if it meant he had a friend for the day. Krynn looked like a little blue bird herself, standing on the branch like she was, her long blue dress fluttering around her ankles, and her brown curls sticking out like feathers.

"Are there any nests in this tree?" he asked.

Krynn nodded happily and pointed. "Right up there. And there are three eggs inside. We should probably leave so the mother can come back to sit on them."

Joran glanced at the branch above them, and sure enough, a small brown conglomeration of twigs nestled in the crook of wood.

He jumped down and Krynn followed, her movements graceful, even in her long dress.

"Is there anywhere you haven't looked?" he asked.

"I haven't looked around the pond for a while," she chirped. "I was here last month, but it was still too early for the skylarks to be back."

He followed her, helplessly lost as she chattered about birds he had never heard of, wishing he could find a nest for her, but not knowing what to look for. She was walking carefully, gently pushing back the tall grass around the edge of the water and scanning the ground.

"There are birds who build nests on the ground?" He sounded skeptical.

Krynn giggled and Joran's eyes darted to hers as he smiled too.

"Of course. Especially around water like this. There are skylarks, nightjars, lapwings," she counted the birds off on her fingers.

Joran's eyes fell and he dropped to his knees. He had spotted brown grass under the green leaves of a tall weed. Pushing back the green, he gasped as his eyes fell on five brown eggs lying in the hollow of the dried grass nest. His heart beat faster with excitement, but his happiness was nothing compared with Krynn's.

She crouched beside him, peering into the nest. He caught her expression as her mouth fell open and she gaped at him in amazement. "You did it! You found a skylark nest with five babies!"

The awe in her voice awakened a strange feeling in his chest. He sat back on his heels, gazing at his new friend and smiling like a jester. He couldn't remember a time when he had done anything that had made him feel so good.

***

That night his mother stopped by his bed after the nursemaid had tucked him in.

"You found something to do after all, didn't you? I had to send Alma after you for dinner."

He nodded, drowsily. "I met a girl whose mother works for Lady Marty. She knows a lot about birds. We found four nests and three had eggs in them. I found the skylark one by the pond," he murmured, still basking in the happiness of the afternoon.

Queen Lilian quirked an eyebrow at him. "You played with a servant girl?" Disdain coated her tone.

Joran roused. He wanted to shake his head. He hadn't played with a servant girl. He had played with Krynn. But he couldn't do it, because his mother was right. Krynn was a lady' maid's daughter. His mother's disappointment crashed into his own denial, and he burrowed under the covers. The happy feelings vanished.

CHAPTER THREE

Present

Joran stumbled into his father's study, pushed from behind by Dunn and the others. He used his sleeve to clear his face. They could have let him wash up first.

The King turned slowly. Joran hardly recognized his father. The past two weeks had brought a lot of changes, and he was still processing them. One change was in his father, the way his eyes were darker, more serious and focused. Joran had rarely seen him like that for years, especially not when he had needed him most. The King had regularly been under the Queen's controlling power. It was her means to rule the kingdom, since ancient laws against female reign forbade her from ever having the throne.

"Where were you tonight, Joran?" The King began, but didn't wait for an answer. "You nearly killed yourself the night of the revolt with whatever vile substance you put in your body. You stomped out of our council meeting the next day. And tonight, when I try to meet with you before I return to Lilt, you've disappeared."

Joran didn't say anything.

"Dunn told me more than a number of things that alarm me," the King continued his lecture.

Curse Dunn, Joran thought of his guard. He was much too tight-skinned. Joran scowled.

"Besides you using illegal drugs – my own son, a buyer of something I would like to rid the kingdom of – and stealing from the treasury to afford it, Dunn admits that you drink yourself sick in common taverns, chase village girls, and find yourself in the middle of brawls, both here and in Lilt."

Joran waited for his father to finish his list of sins.

"You're my son, Joran, currently the only son who can rightfully inherit the throne."

He paused. Joran sniffed, avoiding eye contact. After the revolt at their summer castle, the truth had come out that his older twin brother, Benrid, wasn't really his twin at all. He was the King's firstborn, but he wasn't Queen Lilian's child, which meant he was born outside the royal union, thus ineligible to inherit the throne. When the King returned to Lilt, home to the main castle, he and the council would decide Benrid's fate. Joran's younger brother, Golan, was also a half-brother, Lilian's child from a secret affair. He was still trying to comprehend how twisted his family was.

"Do you think you are on the right path to becoming a ruler, if I were to name you crown prince?" His father demanded.

Joran had never heard his father's voice thunder like that. He had always been mild-mannered.

"Do you?"

Joran shook his head. *I don't want to be King. I don't care about becoming a good ruler,* his thoughts screamed. His mother had been trying to manipulate him onto the throne for years, all for her own benefit, but he was sick of the pressure, even if the position was rightfully his now. Spirits, he could hardly face his own life, let alone bear the weight of a kingdom on his shoulders. The fear made him itch to say something rude.

"I wouldn't be any worse than you were," he said, despite the way he bit his tongue to keep the comment inside. He rubbed his forehead after the comment escaped. The jacin made him bold too.

"I have owned up to my mistakes," King Henry said, no less fiercely. "I know I ruled poorly for many years – but at least it wasn't of my own choosing. You're making these choices, Joran."

Of Oceans and Pearls

"I've been making these choices for years," Joran said evenly. "You can change overnight because the spell disappeared. I can't change that easily, and I'm not convinced I want to." At least this was the truth.

Joran was taken aback by the heavy slap across his cheek. His skin burned from the impact. The blood that had clotted began to trickle slowly again. Moisture sprung into his eyes, but not as much from the sting on his skin as from the pain that shot into his heart.

He trembled as he looked into his father's face.

"All I see before me is a nearly grown man acting like a spoiled boy, a man who cares for no one but himself," the King said.

"You haven't *seen* me for years, Father," Joran shot back. "You don't know anything about me. You couldn't help me when I needed you the most. You – "

"I see enough now, Joran!" King Henry cut him off. "I see someone I am ashamed to call mine."

The words stung.

Joran tightened his jaw. His head hurt. His heart hurt. He felt the pouch of jacin in his pocket, longing for the blissful cloud another sniff would bring.

"I've discussed this with the Great Magister and we've decided on a course of action for you. You're leaving tonight, making it to the river by morning, where you will sail through Terind to the sea. From there, you will join Captain Markus' command. He's a military captain whom you will serve under for the next year."

"Wait, you're sending me away?"

King Henry sighed. "Yes. I'm sending you to be someone else's responsibility because I have failed."

"A military ship? I've already been to the Academy." His two years of military training had ended just after Krynn's death.

"A patrol ship, actually. Captain Markus retired from the military, but he still works with the Terindian guard to protect Terind's borders. It will do you good, I hope."

Joran's mind was reeling. Before he could form another question, his father walked away, leaving him standing alone in the dim study.

***

The night had been miserable. Besides having to sit upright on a horse all night surrounded by guards, one of whom held a lead on his horse just in case he decided to bolt, he had been tormented by his father's words. By the time they reached the capital city of Lilt, the sun had already risen. They didn't even stop at the castle there, which was his home when he wasn't spending summers in Rivence.

Benrid, his older brother, was there, and he wasn't even aware yet of everything that had happened in the revolt at Blackstone Castle, where the rest of the family had spent the summer. King Henry and Erlich, the Great Magister, were probably already on the road heading this way. By tomorrow this time, Benrid would know everything. The whole kingdom would know. But Joran would already be gone.

They passed the castle, heading to the river. Joran struggled to push his fear down when he saw the riverboats. This was real. He was being forced away from his home. His family, as flawed as it was. His own kingdom. It was all he knew, and he was leaving all of it.

Joran watched Dunn approach one of the docked ships, his steps weary. He was back in just a few minutes. He motioned for Joran to dismount, which he did, wincing. His bruises were ripe now, and hours in the saddle had made him stiff. Dunn held his arm like he was a criminal, marching him straight up the gangplank. Rodavan followed with a saddlebag with a few of his things.

Dunn jerked his arm, forcing him to look up. "This is your new guard," he said, staring at a slight young man who was regarding them seriously. "I, and the rest of your guards, will be glad for the break." There was no humor in his tone. "Captain Cohen will oversee your transfer to Captain Markus when you reach the sea. Goodbye."

He pushed Joran forward, spun on his heel, and stomped down the ramp.

A sudden panic gripped Joran. He couldn't do this. He would be truly and utterly alone. Dunn had been his guard since he was a boy, and though he didn't love his guard's strict manners, he couldn't remember being without him. Everything he knew was behind him. Off this vessel. Without thinking, he leaped toward the railing. He was a good swimmer.

Something barreled into him from behind, knocking him down. He used his hands to break his fall, but stayed down when he felt a dagger at his back.

"Sorry about that, Prince, but I've been given a job, and it's to keep you safe. And keep you here," a voice said.

He turned his head to see his new guard looking down at him.

Surely things couldn't get any worse.

CHAPTER FOUR

Five years ago

Joran woke on the morning of his fourteenth birthday, the one he shared with Benrid, anticipating the day ahead. Queen Lilian had been planning their joint celebration for months. He had heard her tell his father that he and his brother were old enough that they should begin looking for wives to betrothe to them, but that she would need to vet all the eligible women herself.

"We'll start this year. We can have a huge festival in the boys' honor and invite as many people as this city will hold, from Ethereal and beyond. I'll plan a week's worth of activities - feasts, game tournaments, challenges, and performances. That will give me a bit of time to scope out only the best for the future king."

The thought of being betrothed filled Joran with equal parts curiosity and embarrassment, but his mother hadn't said it would happen this year, only that she needed to start looking. People had been arriving all week, and an encampment had sprung up along the river, tents lining the riverbank as far as he could see.

Carts were still crowding the roads, as they had been for days while people flocked to Lilt for the celebration. The black, silver-rimmed flags of Ethereal rippled from the castle gates and hung from the balconies. Many of the tents boasted the colors of Ethereal, though green and gold banners from Terind, and the light blue mountain crest of Cleft, dotted the scene as well. The early summer breeze caught the banners and tent flaps, creating a dizzying sensation of color and movement below as Joran stopped at his window to gaze at the scene beyond the castle gates.

Even at this early hour, the castle grounds were bustling. The roasting spits had been roaring since yesterday, and the brewery was carting all the barrels they'd stored for months to the riverbank to be distributed freely among the guests.

There was no time waste. The games would begin today. There would be sparring and fencing matches, hand-to-hand combat, and archery contests. Joran couldn't wait to watch the archers. Instead of target boards, they would be shooting moving targets – live, penned animals who were being herded. Prizes would be awarded based on the size of the animal and how close the shots were to death blows. Lyken, Captain of the Guard, would be competing. He was famous for his archery skills. He had already been training Benrid and Joran, and Joran could not wait to see his hero win. Besides, he had gotten wind that he and his brother would be given their own longbows today. His palms prickled with excitement.

***

The fencing matches in the morning had been brilliant. Joran felt his voice already going hoarse from cheering. Lunch was a truly mammoth affair, with tables laden with roasted meat and bread spread for hundreds of yards, all provided by the royal family. Lines formed and people took their meals to grass to enjoy, like a colossal picnic. Joran enjoyed the freedom of this day, a day dedicated to him, a day on which he could do no wrong. He kept his guard frantic as he dashed from table to table, loading his plate with all the best foods, including more desserts than he would have been allowed in a week.

Archery was scheduled for that afternoon. To Joran's surprise, there had been an announcement that after the men competed, there would be a young man's contest as well. He fully intended to join. Lyken said he was a natural. If he had received his gift by then, he could even use his new bow for the competition. Not that Lyken would approve. "You have to know your weapon," he always said, but Joran knew he wouldn't be able to keep from showing it off.

Everyone he passed murmured their congratulations, and though he enjoyed the attention, it was getting hard to respond every time. He barely nodded, not even glancing at the person who called, "Happy birthday, Prince Joran!"

His mouth was already full, and he was looking for a place to enjoy his feast.

"Lady Marty deserves more respect than that," Dunn whispered at his elbow.

Joran's head shot up. He knew that name. He scanned the people in the direction from which the voice had come. A tall, older woman was smiling dutifully at him, and he grinned and nodded in return, but he wasn't looking at her at all.

Krynn!

He spotted her a few steps behind Lady Marty. She caught his gaze and smiled shyly.

Joran's stomach flip-flopped, but he managed a wink. Then he wandered on, only circling back from behind after a few minutes. He came up behind her, safely hidden from Lady Marty's view, and cleared his throat. Krynn spun, her face a mask of bashfulness, but a smile tugging at her lips all the same.

Joran felt a wave of his own timidness wash over him. Krynn was much taller than when he'd met her — even taller than him by a bit, and her hair was long. The barely-brown curls trailed past her shoulders. She looked nearly grown up.

He pushed his sudden shyness away with a goofy smile. He leaned toward her and whispered conspiratorially, "I heard there is a blind archer scheduled for this afternoon. He won't even know what he's missing." He winked again.

Her pale-blue eyes widened, and then she spurted a laugh.

"Have you eaten?"

She shook her head.

He held up his own food. "I've already found the best tables. I can show you."

She glanced toward Lady Marty and another woman standing beside her.

"I'll have to let my mother know," she said.

A few minutes later, she joined him. He showed her how to skip the lines by coming up to the tables from the back and where to find the custards.

She giggled as he loaded her plate almost as full as his. "I could never eat this all at once. No more!"

They found a spot and sank into the soft grass.

"You were born at the perfect time of year," she offered. Seeing his question, she explained, "The weather isn't hot, it isn't cold. You can be outside all day long and enjoy every minute of it! I'm so glad I got to come. Lilt is just beautiful." She gestured toward the river in the distance. "Oh, and happy birthday, Your Highness!"

She dropped her eyes again, and this time Joran couldn't think of a joke.

***

"I can't wait to see this," Joran confided to Krynn when the archers were in place. He hadn't let her return to her mother or her mistress yet. It was too much fun showing her the castle.

Her brows bunched together as she scanned the scene. "What are they aiming at? Oh, please, no. Not those animals?"

"Yes, the idea of a live, moving target seemed more difficult. See the man with the blue cap? That's Lyken, Captain of our royal guard. He's my instructor. I have no doubt he will win today."

Krynn's face hadn't smoothed. "But the animals. They're going to die?"

"Well, yes, probably. Most of them. But the edible ones will be cooked for the feast tomorrow."

She paled. "I don't think I can watch," she whispered.

Joran blinked. "You can't watch the archers?"

"I can't watch the animals suffer."

He glanced at the animals in the pen. They were mostly hogs. He hadn't given their lives a thought, but now that he thought about how much they would squeal, he didn't want Krynn to be there. If she was this distressed just at the thought...

"Do you want to see the lake?" he asked.

She brightened. Then, "No, Your Highness, you don't have to leave because of me. I'll go back to Lady Marty."

He didn't want her to leave. Much as he wanted to see the archery, he wanted to spend time with her. He had been planning on joining the later contest, but if she couldn't bear to watch, it would take all the fun out of it for him. In fact, she was the only one he cared about seeing him right now. After he received his gift, he would take her somewhere she could watch him aim at trees. Having decided, he turned to her.

"You can call me Joran, and I actually feel more like swimming than shooting today," he tossed back, already walking toward the lake.

***

True to his word, Joran stripped out of his shoes and shirt when they reached the lake, and with a shout, dove under the water. When he came up for air, Krynn was grinning from the edge. He splashed at her, and she laughed, scrambling back.

When he joined her on the bank, she glanced at his dripping pants. "Your mother must hate how often you ruin your good clothes."

He laughed. "More like the laundry women, but with three boys at the castle, they expect it."

He sobered, realizing how obvious he had just made their social classes.

He changed the subject. "I know how to find skylark nests now. I've even found a few other kinds from time to time, but I don't know the birds like you do."

She looked surprised. "You remember?"

"Of course." He made a face. "You saved me from a really boring afternoon that day."

"Well," she smiled. "You might have to show me. It's possible they're still nesting now. I hardly ever get to go to the estate anymore. Too many responsibilities at home. I sew for milady now."

They were interrupted by a guard jogging his way toward them. "Your Highness! You need to get to the address balcony. The King and Queen are ready to present your gifts. They're waiting on you," he panted.

Joran stood and threw his shirt on, over his head. He brushed the grass off his soaking wet pants, and ran a hand through his dripping hair. He threw Krynn a mischievous grin. "Don't go anywhere," he told her. "I want to show you something when I get back."

***

Joran wasn't disappointed. There on the center balcony, above everyone, his father and mother presented him and Benrid with exquisitely crafted longbows. Even Lyken, who owned a myriad of weapons, would envy this one, Joran knew, as he held the polished wood in his hands. It was full-sized too, and that made Joran proud.

As soon as he could get away, he rushed back to the lake, the young archers contest long forgotten. He breathed a sigh of relief when he saw Krynn still sitting there, leaning back on her hands.

She jumped up when she saw him. "Oh, that's beautiful!" she exclaimed, noticing the bow over his shoulder right away.

"I can't wait to try it," he admitted. "Will you watch me practice?"

"Mother will scold me tonight for being gone so long, but I would love to watch you shoot. It looks heavy. Is it?"

"You can hold it," he offered. He placed the bow in her arms.

After a few shots, which he was quite pleased with, Krynn said, "You make it look easy."

"It's not all that hard, and I have been training for two years. Why don't you try?"

"Really?"

He loved the excitement lacing her voice. He placed the bow back in her hands, helping her position it, and handed her an arrow.

"Line up that notch with your target," he instructed. "Wherever that notch is when you let go is where the arrow will end up."

She nocked the arrow, but the taut bowstring wouldn't budge.

"Here." He stood on the other side of her, his arms encircling her to steady the bow and pull the string for her.

He caught a whiff of jasmine in her hair. He was surprised by how soft she felt against him. Distracted, he let go a second too late, sending her well-aimed arrow teetering toward the ground only a few feet away.

He laughed nervously and took a step back. "Sorry. I guess timing doesn't work as well that way."

Something he had never felt before welled up inside him. He wondered how to hide what he was feeling, and then wondered if he ever wanted the feeling to go away.

CHAPTER FIVE

Present

Joran had risen with the sun and was standing on the deck, gaping at the scene before him. The mouth of the river had widened, and they were docked at a port in Kestell. He'd never been to this part of Terind, and was surprised that the city was busy, even at dawn. He had never seen so much activity, even in Lilt. The port was lined with sailing vessels. Some were small fishing boats, but most were much larger than the riverboat he was on, grand ships that lived at sea. Crew members scurried about the ships, and the dock itself was a mass of color and movement. Fishermen unloaded their catch, carting fish away to the market, and sailors carried supplies from town to their respective ships. The most amazing part of all, though, was the sea itself.

Joran had grown up on a lake, and he had traveled on the River Lilt before, for which their capital was named, but he had never seen such an expanse of water. The deep-blue ripples stretched as far as he could see. Nothing but water and sky. He felt dwarfed.

Captain Cohen ambled up beside him. "You transfer to the Pearl today. Are you ready?"

Joran hadn't spoken to the Captain much, and the man didn't seem overly eager to speak to him either. He was probably relieved to be getting rid of him. Same as most people. Even his new guard, Peter, had been maddeningly quiet, although he shadowed Joran closely. Joran considered running again. It would be easy to get lost here, but it would not change the fact that he was unwelcome at home, or that he was all alone in a new place. Besides, he suddenly felt another pair of eyes on him and knew Peter had joined them.

He shrugged and nodded at the Captain.

***

The metallic scent in the air grew thicker as they approached the wharves. It was a new smell, the smell of the sea, and Joran tried not to wrinkle his nose against it. The Pearl towered above her mooring, the chipping, black-painted planks creaking as it rocked in the shallow water. So, this was to be his prison for a year.

Captain Markus met him on deck. He nodded his thanks to Captain Cohen, who left as hurriedly as Dunn had. Joran sized up the Captain. He wasn't tall, but he stood as straight as a pole. His white beard was trimmed close to his face, and his eyes were piercing.

He studied Joran before his eyes flicked to Peter and back.

"I've been expecting you, Your Highness. The messenger arrived a few days ago with a message from your father. Welcome aboard the Pearl. Who accompanies you?"

Peter stepped forward when Joran scowled. "I'm Peter Kent, royal guard."

Captain Markus gave a single nod.

"Well, we've been waiting on you and the tide this morning. Now that you're here, we should sail in an hour's time. Your Highness, from this point on, you will be addressed as Joran. On the King's desires, you will become one of my crew and treated as such. You will be expected to pull your share of the workload, just like anyone else. Of course, from what I've been told, you will probably spend more of your time spewing than anything else, for the first few days at least. The first mate has offered you his cabin until you adjust. Then you will sleep below decks with the rest of the crew."

Joran's stomach clenched.

"Also, I'll need to conduct a personal search. Please empty your pockets."

The flicker of dread that danced in his stomach burst into flame. His mind raced for a way to conceal the jacin and the other drugs he had stashed. Spirits, if they were sailing in an hour, he barely had time to stock up on more before they left. This was a new city. It would take some time to locate dealers. He couldn't afford to lose what he had.

"Joran! I expect complete and immediate compliance." Captain Markus signaled two sailors. They gripped Joran's arms.

Anger surged up. He was tired of being hauled around like a mule. He cursed.

"Fine," he said tightly. "Let me go."

The men slowly released his arms. Joran threw the pouch of jacin and the other two drugs at the Captain's feet.

"Peter, hand me all the belongings. I'll go through them and bring them to your cabin shortly. Kirk will show you to his cabin where you will be staying for a few days." Captain Markus reached for the drugs and tossed them deftly into the water.

Joran's skin burned.

Kirk motioned them forward, opening a low door. The cabin was small and bare.

"I don't envy you your imminent headache," he said without malice, closing the door behind them and leaving Joran and Peter in silence.

Joran threw himself back on the bunk and rubbed his forehead. Panic was threatening, but he had to think. He had to get off this ship. Curse Peter. He was like a silent predator, his black eyes always following Joran. There was no way he would let him get off the ship right now, let alone find drugs in the city.

"That's dangerous stuff," Peter commented, as if reading his thoughts. "You'll be better for getting off it." He was arranging a pile of ropes in the corner.

Joran glared at his back. "Hey, prison guard, can you go see if this blasted ship has any food? We've been up for hours and haven't eaten." If he could get out of Peter's sight, just for a minute, he might be able to escape.

Peter sank onto the ropes. "Once we set sail, I'll find out. I'm hungry too."

Joran groaned. "I thought you were supposed to take care of me."

"Protect you. There's a difference."

He hated the young man's unperturbed manner. It was infuriating.

"I'm the Prince," he tried again.

"And I work for your father," Peter replied easily.

"Seriously, are you going to be at my heels for the next year? I don't need a puppy." He let his annoyance coat his tone.

"I plan on it."

Joran felt like the walls of his life that had toppled over when Krynn had died, had been crumbling ever since, and today, the rubble was burying him. He was trapped on a floating prison with a captain who was as stern and unfriendly as Dunn. There was no way to restock his jacin supply, and nothing to use in the meantime, and now he was going to be shadowed by a prudish guard.

"Then I plan on making it the most miserable year of your life," he promised Peter.

***

Several hours later, Joran had forgotten about food and everything else. He had never been so sick. His head pounded; he was sure it was splitting in two. He could hardly see, he was so dizzy and achy. The ship hurdled up and down the ocean waves, which were much stronger and deeper than any river currents, making his stomach heave. He had already lost count of how many times he had vomited into the bucket beside his cot. Chills followed by burning skin chased each other all over his body, making him shake uncontrollably.

Peter was affected too, but he kept his agony silent, disappearing on deck when he needed to be sick.

The ship's physician came to check on Joran. He pursed his lips. "Miserable few days you've got ahead of you. The seasickness on top of the withdrawals, not gonna be easy."

He placed his hand on Joran's clammy, sweat-soaked face. "Take some of this, boy. It's got ginger - may help your stomach. Regardless, you need to keep swallowing. I've seen men dry out and die quicker'n you'd 'spect when they get the sickness like this."

Joran wanted nothing more than to die, but he tried to swallow the spicy liquid the doctor poured into his mouth. It came back up only a few minutes later.

***

On the third day, the pain in his head had eased into a dull ache in his temples. His stomach still hurt, but he had managed to keep his last drink down for the past few hours. Spirits, he smelled bad. He rubbed his forehead and looked around. The cabin was still and quiet in the daylight. While he'd hovered between reality and delirium the past few days, he'd seen frightening images in here. The walls warped and grew evil faces, crowding closer and closer. Bats had dived toward him, and he had screamed, only to open his eyes a moment later and see nothing but the oil lamp rocking from the ceiling.

His eyes now fell on Peter, who had claimed the pile of ropes as his bed, a blanket spread over them. He was kneeling in front of his makeshift bunk now, his head bent. He must have felt Joran's eyes, because he looked back a moment later. The smallest hint of a smile passed over his expression.

"You're awake and not throwing up," he commented.

Joran grunted.

"Beginning to feel better?"

He shrugged. He still felt like rubbish, but not as bad as he had.

"You've already been keeping your promise, by the way," Peter continued, the smile touching his lips again.

Joran looked at him sharply. He wasn't expecting humor from this boy.

"What are you doing?" he asked, glancing at his kneeling position skeptically.

"Oh. I was praying," Peter said, rising to his feet.

Joran choked. "So not only am I shackled with a guard who won't leave me alone, or listen to me, but now a praying one?"

"Every morning," Peter rejoined. "And now I think I'll go check on that food you asked about last week." He ducked, disappearing out the door.

CHAPTER SIX

Three years ago

The birthday celebration for the twin princes became an annual event. Krynn came every year, and every year Joran slunk away from the crowds to spend time bird-watching and swimming with her. He never joined the archery contests, although he trained all year long. He was competent with his bow now. His skill was Lyken's pride. Last year, when they turned fifteen, Benrid had won second place in the contest. Something like that would typically upset Joran; he and his twin were not close in the usual way twins were. They didn't get along and turned everything into a competition, without the friendliness of sport. The win upset his mother, who never liked it when Benrid got more attention than Joran. She urged Joran to enter this year, but he laughed and told her he wanted to give the others a fair chance.

She didn't know about Krynn. He hadn't forgotten her comment the first day he had met Krynn six years before. Joran didn't care that Benrid had placed in the archery contest. He could have the honor; he didn't have Krynn.

"My mother knows I'm spending the day with you," Krynn admitted now. She was perched beside him on the branch of a tree.

"Was she upset?"

"Of course. You're the Prince. She said…" Krynn chewed the corner of her mouth, avoiding Joran's gaze.

He could guess what she had said. It wasn't healthy for her seamstress daughter to be running around all day with the Prince of Ethereal. They weren't children anymore. Servants weren't *friends* with royalty.

He sighed. "She's just worried for you."

"I know."

They were silent. There wasn't anything to say. Joran didn't want to give her up. He looked forward to this week of the year more than any other time, and not because he got a gift or was admired. He liked the thrill of sneaking away from his guards. He enjoyed being carefree. He enjoyed showing Krynn his life. He enjoyed *her*.

He cast a sideways glance at her. Her curly, light-brown hair had turned to rippling waves which swung near her waist now. She always wore it loose down her back, usually covered by a scarf, but the scarf had come loose and fallen off earlier. He'd shoved the material in his pocket when it fell, secretly thrilled to gaze at her without it. Her periwinkle-blue eyes were framed with dark lashes. She was the prettiest girl he had ever met. His heart tightened painfully.

Things were changing. Surely someone would notice Krynn now, and she would be married off. She was sixteen. It could happen any day. And he was leaving next month for military training at the Academy. He would be gone for two years at the least.

He didn't know when they would see each other again.

And he thought he might be falling in love with her.

He gulped.

Golan came running toward them. When he spotted them, he called, "Dunn is furious that he can't find you. And now Mother is looking for you. If you don't go soon, you'll get yourself and your guard in trouble."

His eyes darted to Krynn, openly curious. Joran slid out of the tree, landing lightly on his feet. Golan, a few years younger, annoyed the life out of him, but he forced an easy smile as he gave Krynn a hand down.

"Tell Dunn I'll be right there, and stall Mother, will you? I need to escort Lady Astrior back to her family first."

Golan gave them a quick nod and left. Joran caught the blush spreading up Krynn's neck. He knew she had never been called Lady Astrior before. She probably wasn't comfortable with the lie, but Golan was much too straightforward to hide their secret. Joran couldn't have his mother finding out that he was still enchanted with the servant girl. Queen Lilian was determined to find him a princess. She hadn't been satisfied with anyone yet, and every year it was a relief. If she ever pushed a betrothal, he would have to tell her the truth. While he could enjoy these moments without tainting them with reality, he would.

"I'd better go," he looked apologetically at Krynn.

She twisted a flower stem in her hands and gave him a sad smile. "I know."

He leaned closer to whisper, "Don't worry about your mother. She's just afraid her little bird might become a princess if she hangs around a prince too much." It had started off as a joke, but as the words came out, he realized what he was saying.

Krynn did too because the blush spread up her face.

The scent of jasmine filled his nostrils, and his heart tripped. He reached out, gently touching his fingertips to the red on her cheek. A thrill shot through him at the contact. His hurry was forgotten as he realized how enchanting it was to stand this close to her. He let his fingers slide down her jaw. She lifted her big, blue eyes to his, causing his insides to melt. Slowly, hesitantly, he leaned toward her mouth. She didn't pull back.

Their lips met, so softly at first, it felt like a whisper. Then hers parted, and his mouth was with hers, in hers. They were one. Her lips were so soft.

He groaned. She was heaven.

Finally she nudged him back with a hand on his chest. He pulled away, his gaze resting on her pillowy lips before falling to her hand over his heart. It rose and fell rapidly with his breathing.

"You need to go," she whispered.

He met her eyes, slowly breaking into a devilish half-grin. "In a minute. That was too much fun." He sank his mouth onto hers again.

Spirits, he didn't want to go anywhere. He wanted to stay here all day. Finally he straightened and tossed his blond hair back, unable to stop the smile stretching across his face.

Krynn smiled too, but hesitantly. "Thank you," she breathed. "I'm very lucky to have my first kiss from a prince." She kept her eyes carefully averted, though her cheeks flushed.

He hardly noticed. He was too happy. Throwing his head back, he put an arm around her waist and twirled them in a circle. "And all the rest of your kisses shall be from a prince too because I'm in love with you, Krynn Astrior!"

She was shaking her head, and it caused the tears pooled in her eyes to slip down her cheeks. He stopped. "What's wrong?"

"I can't, I mean, you are?'" There was such hope and fear tangled in her features that her expression tore at his heart.

He took her face gently in his hands, the way he had been longing to for a while. Now that he'd touched her, he was eager to do it again. His thumbs brushed the tears away, and he gazed into her depthless, blue eyes.

"Yes, Krynn, I love you. I've loved you for years, and I'll love you for the rest of our lives."

A giggle and a sob collided in her throat, and she threw her arms around him, her face buried in his chest.

CHAPTER SEVEN

Present

By day six, Joran awoke feeling almost normal. The room wasn't spinning, anyway. He spotted Peter, praying in his corner again and rolled his eyes. The fellow moved like a serpent, so quietly that he never woke Joran, although he was always up before him.

Peter stood, his back still turned, and said, "Captain says we begin duties today. We're to meet the crew for breakfast and talk to him afterwards."

Joran grunted. Breakfast finally sounded appealing. Ship duties and a conversation with the Captain did not, but he swung his legs over the side of the bunk.

"Oh, and give me those clothes. You can wear something you packed. I'll just have time to wash them before breakfast."

Joran gaped. "I thought you only protected me, not took care of me."

Peter snorted. "Believe me, this is entirely in my own interest. I can't take the stench in here."

Joran scowled, but stripped, handing the offending clothes to Peter who waited with his back turned. Peter tossed them in a bucket and headed to the door. "There's water and soap by the chamber pot," he called.

Joran washed and changed. Spirits, that did help. His face was rough with newly grown beard spikes, but he didn't see a razor. He shrugged. Most of the sailors had beards anyway. Easier this way.

***

The Captain ate with the crew, as though he were one of them. No one paid Joran open attention, though he noticed their interested glances on the sly. The porridge was horrible. It was lumpy, thick, and tasteless, but Joran forced himself to swallow.

"Good to see you on your feet, Joran," Captain Markus greeted him a few minutes later.

"Actually I'm on my backside right now," Joran quipped. Neither Peter nor the Captain smiled.

"You'll be on kitchen duty today with Maniv," he continued, as though Joran hadn't spoken. "We'll rotate your duties weekly, since neither of you have sailing experience. Peter, you'll be helping the deckhands. Your shift ends at dinner. After dinner, both of you retrieve your things from Kirk's cabin and find bunks below decks. Now that your recovery is over, he will be needing his cabin back."

Joran watched the Captain's retreating back, annoyed. He was already tired of being ordered around.

He glared at Peter instead. "At least I won't have to spend the day with you," he shot, hoping for a reaction from his devout guard. Nothing flitted over Peter's expression, who simply cleared his bowl from the table and nodded as he left.

Joran rubbed his forehead. Kitchen duty. He scoffed.

He headed toward the galley. A gag jumped up his throat when he stuck his head inside, and he quickly retreated. He was about to be sick again. He took shallow breaths until he finally had his stomach under control, then tried again. Maniv looked up from the wooden counter this time, his brows lifted in welcome. "Ah, my new recruit. Come, come," he motioned Joran in.

Joran's nose twitched, and he tried not to breathe in. "Why does it reek in here?"

Maniv looked confused.

"It smells like rotten fish," he accused.

Maniv shrugged. "You can empty the waste, but we eat lots of fish. Always smells of fish."

"Great." Already the day was bleak. *At least it won't be much work*, he tried to comfort himself.

His muscles that evening told a different story. He had been on his feet all day. Maniv spoke with an accent that was difficult to understand, and Joran's head was spinning again from listening so intently to make out what he was saying.

He'd hauled water all day long, in between scrubbing dirty breakfast dishes, peeling potatoes, and scouring the floor. His hands were clumsy with the dishes and the knives. It made his skin itch. Holding a dagger, throwing a knife, these things came as easily as breathing. He had been practicing for years. Trying to wield a tiny knife to slice off potato skins was entirely different, and he hated it.

At first Maniv tried to chat, but after being met only by grunts, he fell silent. The day dragged by. Dinner finally came, and Joran left the galley in a huff, the door swinging behind him. He fell into a seat on the long bench.

Peter slid in quietly beside him.

"Did you have a good day?"

Joran snorted. "You don't have to be so polite. In fact, if you really want to make my life better, don't talk to me at all. But, if you want to know, no. I had a horrible day. The kitchen is thick with the smell of rotten fish, the cook has the most annoying accent, and my fingers are stiff from cutting up those bloody potatoes you're eating."

The man on the other side of him nudged him in the ribs and chuckled. "Maniv is the only one who actually enjoys the galley, lad. You're in good company, but we all do our share. At least he didn't have you clean the fish yet, did he?"

He chuckled again, and someone else added, "And at least the fish is fresh. Wait till you start working with the pork brine. They say the salt preserves it, but it smells rancid from the start. Worse is coming, I'll warn you."

Joran wasn't in the mood for teasing, so he swung off the bench, stomping toward the cabin before he did something he might regret.

Peter opened the door a few minutes later. Joran sat on the edge of the cot, elbows on his knees and his head in his hands. Peter pushed a bowl of stew under his nose, and he took it reluctantly.

He peered at Peter from under his lowered brows, noticing the dagger at his waist, and he glared. His own knives were in the Captain's keeping. "How come you get to keep your weapons and mine were confiscated?"

"Guard."

Joran scoffed. "That's unjust. How am I supposed to defend myself without any weapons?"

Peter shot him a glance. "Um, guard," he said again, pointing to himself.

Joran exhaled in frustration and grew sullen. He picked at his food in silence. When he finished, he risked a glance at Peter, who was sitting on the floor, leaning against the wall. One arm rested on a bent knee, the other leg stretched out in front of him. He quickly averted his eyes from Joran's face.

"I wish you would say something sometimes," Joran muttered. Peter's quiet observing was unnerving.

Nothing. Of course. Peter annoyed him when he talked, and he annoyed him when he didn't.

"Don't you ever get mad?"

"I used to."

"Used to? You sound like an old man. You act so wise, like you know everything, but you're not better than me. You're a skinny kid who somehow landed the job of your dreams - a 'royal guard.' Is this what you wanted? To be stuck on a floating prison for a year with someone like me?"

Peter's lips twitched. "No, I can honestly say I didn't foresee this in my career." He stood and picked up his bedding and bag and a stack of papers.

"What are those?" Joran asked.

Peter glanced at the papers, tilting the pile toward Joran. "Pictures. I draw."

The top picture was a sketch of a knotted rope. Two separate ropes interlocked in a tight knot in the middle of the page, every small fiber penciled in. It was good, but Joran rolled his eyes. Peter loved work so much, he drew the blasted ropes for fun.

"I'm heading down," Peter said.

Joran sat for a minute longer, watching Peter leave. He couldn't explain why the guard got on his nerves so badly. *I will get a reaction out of him,* he promised himself.

***

Hammocks hung side by side filling the crew's quarters. Peter motioned Joran to a hammock. "These are ours," he said, indicating two hammocks that nearly touched. There was no privacy here. No space. Joran took a deep breath to calm his irritation and secured his bag with the extra length of rope dropped from the hammock hook. The air smelled almost as bad in here as in the galley. He wrinkled his nose at the stench of sweat and unwashed feet and wondered if Peter was going to start doing everyone's laundry. The thought made him smirk.

He heard chatter and laughter coming from the stairs dropping deeper into the ship and he wandered over, crouching to see down. About twelve of the crew were relaxing around three small tables. Lanterns swung blithely from above, glinting off the tin mugs. Joran could smell the ale, and a craving gnawed at his middle. He jogged down the stairs, sliding into a chair near the wall.

This felt familiar. He smiled and reached for a mug.

"Not tonight, mate. Captain's orders," Kirk said easily.

Joran narrowed his eyes.

"No drinking for you for a while, that's all," he said again. His tone was light, but there was a spark of authority in his eyes that made Joran set the mug down.

He clenched his jaw, but was distracted from his anger by a chubby sailor who rolled to his feet. "My turn," he announced. His words slurred just a bit. "The best kiss I ever got was from a pixie."

The others howled, and Serb, the tall, black-haired man Joran had seen the first day, pulled him down by his arm, laughing.

"No such thing," someone said.

The man tried standing again, but was waved down.

"Nah, Pillows, no good. Only real tales tonight."

Joran perked up.

"Best kiss? I've got one," he offered, his charming smirk in place.

"Let's hear from the new lad," Kirk smiled.

"You're too young for the ladies," Pillows complained.

"And you're too much for them," Serb roared, playfully slapping his friend's expansive stomach. "Besides, it's the young ones who get all the pretty ones." He waggled his eyebrows at Joran. "Right?"

Joran laughed. "I was in a tavern when the prettiest girl walked in. She was way too beautiful for that place - rosy lips, yellow curls, all sweet and round in the right places - so I walked up to her. I was worried about her, you know."

He paused to let the men chuckle.

"She was looking for her grandfather. I told her I'd escort her - can't have a lady alone in a place like that. She took my arm, just like a proper lady. I swear, every man in there shot a jealous look my way. She finally spotted her grandfather a few tables away. He hadn't seen her yet, so I told her I had never had the privilege of escorting a lady as fine as her, and I would be forever honored if she would grace me with just one kiss for my efforts." He raised an eyebrow. "I can be quite a beggar."

Even Pillows laughed.

"She acted shy at first, but then she said, 'It would be a pleasure. Close your eyes,' and I did. I've learned never to trust a woman since then. I gave her the most modest little kiss so I wouldn't scare her away, and I opened my eyes to see how she liked it. She had bumped into me a bit roughly, so I knew she hadn't had any practice. When I opened my eyes, I was staring face-to-face with her grandfather. He wiped his lips, looked at me oddly, and then slapped me."

The men hooted.

"Wait, you mean you kissed the old man?"

"I did. Believe me, I was rubbing my lips raw trying to get the feeling off. I gave the little lady a withering look, but she grabbed my arm. 'Please don't be mad,' she said, and it was hard to feel anything but desire when I looked at her closely like that. 'I couldn't kiss you in front of him, and he was right next to me. I didn't mean to push him, I was just a bit flustered. As soon as I get him headed toward home, I'll meet you outside in the back for a real kiss if you want.'"

Kirk shook his head. "She did not. Don't make up tales."

"Sure as the spirits she did. I found out she wasn't as innocent as she looked. Those kisses were well practiced." He winked, and the conversation carried on.

When he finally clambered into his swinging bed, he noticed Peter watching him.

"Was that a true story?" he asked.

"What story? Oh, the one I told the men?"

Peter nodded.

"It was true enough." He turned his back, signaling the end of the conversation, though he could feel Peter's thoughts. *True enough, except that it wasn't the best kiss I've had.* He blinked in the semi-darkness, his suspended bed rocking gently, and willed sleep to come.

CHAPTER EIGHT

Two years ago

A year had passed at the military academy when Joran and Benrid were allowed their first holiday home. There hadn't been a birthday celebration this year. Even though they were royalty, spring found them in the thick of examinations, and they weren't exempt.

At seventeen, Joran had stretched into a man. The daily training and exercises had developed his muscles, which corded and tightened as he moved. He was lithe and comfortable in his body. The training for focus and precision had enhanced his already light personality into an easy-mannered, well-spoken person. Benrid had also grown, and his skill with his bow almost matched Joran's. The fire between the twins had eased somewhat once they left home. They still weren't close, but in keeping their distance, they kept their relationship afloat.

Two weeks. That's all the time off he had, and Joran was battling sleep as he tried to come up with a plan to see Krynn. They wrote constantly. She addressed him simply as Joran on the letters, and he addressed her as Lady Astrior. Their communication was no secret, at least not at the Academy, but no one knew who the mysterious Lady Astrior was, and they held Joran in some awe for his secret relationship. He knew that Krynn's mother knew too, and that she still disapproved - not enough to stop Krynn, but enough to worry. He understood why, of course, but one day she would see. He would marry Krynn and it would no longer matter that she had been born a servant. So far, Krynn and her mother had intercepted all his letters before Lady Marty saw them.

He and Benrid were expected to travel home together. If he didn't, he would have to explain to Benrid, and Benrid would certainly tell their parents. He knew Queen Lilian would never approve regardless of Krynn's station. She was extremely particular about his future, even with eligible young women. It was two days home, and another two days further to Lady Marty's. Once there, what excuse could he make to be visiting? He hardly knew the noblewoman.

And there was no way Krynn could get free to meet him. Her mother would never cover for her, even if he arranged the trip. She was constantly busy with her sewing and other duties, and her employer would notice her absence.

He rubbed his forehead and punched his pillow, tired, but annoyed that he couldn't think of anything. He had to see her. He knew that much. He couldn't wait another year to kiss her again.

***

Dear Krynn,

I am beyond thankful I was able to see you, if only for a few hours. It was worth every minute of pretending to be ill and every second of bouncing on a saddle like a madman once Benrid had left for home. Thank you for coming to meet me. I didn't want to put you in danger of getting in trouble. I don't ever want to put you in danger. I don't think I could have gone another day without kissing you. I looked forward to it all year. Every time you sent a letter, I held it and savored the feel of the paper just as much as when I read it because I imagined your pretty fingers holding the quill and folding the paper and blowing your kisses into it - like a fairy, as you say.

But those letters were nothing compared to the real you. If we could have spent every minute of my two weeks together, I would not have gotten tired of holding you. I would have kissed you all day and all night and never slept. Spirits, you keep me awake more than you know. You are so beautiful, Krynn. I can't believe the One blessed me to meet you when we were children.

My holiday home was good. It was nice to be home again, although my mother and father seemed distant. My father was more absent-minded than ever. Maybe it's just his age. It made

Of Oceans and Pearls

me kind of sad, to be honest. Golan has finally grown up a bit. Mostly I couldn't stop thinking of you, so I'm sorry if I don't have much else to say.

I love you, Birdie. Never change.

Yours,

Joran

My dear Joran,

Meeting you in the woods was the most exciting thing I've ever done. I can't believe I was actually brave enough to crawl out the window in the dark to see you. I'm so glad I made it, even if I was terrified the whole time that my mother would wake up and find me gone. Your kisses made me forget that for a while though. I love you, and I can't even tell you how much, because there are no words to explain it.

I'm glad you got to go home for a bit. Did you get to show Lyken how much you have improved? I bet you are his equal now.

I was commissioned to sew a wedding dress this week. I've never made something so important, or so detailed before. It's dark-blue velvet, and I love working on it because the fabric is soft on my fingers. It feels like working with clouds. It reminds me of the sky at twilight, when the world is going to sleep. There are yards of lace to attach, and so many embroidered details, but I get to use golden thread, which is also very pretty.

I love you now and forever, my Prince. My Joran.

Yours,

Krynn

***

Between the letters and studying and the physical practice, the year was flying by. Joran was on track to graduate in four months. Then he would be free to marry Krynn. He practiced his conversation with his mother and father almost daily. He knew they would be unhappy, but Queen Lilian had always favored him and given in to whatever he wanted. He had no doubt she would eventually give in to this as well. After all, she only wanted him to be happy. She had said so many times. Besides, he was at the top of his class. Even Benrid hadn't scored quite as well as he did, and that would pull his mother's favor, he knew.

Then he got the letter.

Joran,

I have terrible news. I don't know what to do. I'm going to be up before sunrise to post this letter. I need your help. I pray this reaches you faster than ever before.

I'm getting married. It happened so suddenly. First, Lady Marty found one of your letters. My mother tried to protect us. She suggested it must be a different Joran, and that it was a harmless infatuation, but Lady Marty saw that it was from the

Academy. Your mother visited with your Aunt Adeline two months ago and mentioned you're there. Lady Marty wrote to Queen Lilian immediately, and just a few days later, the Queen appeared for an unexpected visit.

It was peculiar. She acted odd, and I almost believe she did something to Lady Marty because I have never seen Milady act so strangely. It confused my mother too. By that evening, Lady Marty told me that she had chosen a husband for me, and we were to be married in a month. A month, Joran!

To think that I rejoiced to make a wedding dress. Now I'm supposed to be making my own - a much less grand affair, of course - and it is the worst thing I have ever done. I keep bursting into tears. My mother finally told me to stop altogether and she will finish it. She is even less happy with this arranged marriage than she was with you. At least she could tell you and I cared about each other. Neither of us know this other man. She's worried for me and worried that I will be taken from her, but what else can we do? No one would hire outcasts from an upstanding family like Lady Marty's if we left her employ.

My heart is breaking. I am so afraid. I will run away if I have to, but I don't know where I would go, and I want you to be able to find me. I will wait as long as I can for your reply. Please hurry, and please help me.

I love you. Forever.

Krynn

Of Oceans and Pearls

The breath had left Joran's lungs. His fingertips felt cold, and the paper shook between them. A storm had hindered the mail last week. He peeked at the date and his stomach sank with dread. Almost two weeks ago.

The mail had finally arrived that morning and he had been eager for his, taking it back to his room to go through before his first class. Now his class was about to begin, and he couldn't move.

He sank to the floor, trying to force himself to read the words again and think, but they scalded his eyes. His gaze fell to the other missive in his hand. Cold fingers curled around his heart. This one was from his mother.

My dearest son,

I'm writing this to you tonight, before I leave in the morning to pay Lady Marty a visit. As you know, she's a close friend of my sister's and lives near her. She alerted me recently that she found a letter in her mail from you, addressed to "Lady Astrior." It's strange. The only "Astriors" at that address are a seamstress servant girl and her mother.

Joran, this cannot possibly be the little girl you met at the estate years ago when I took you with me one year, can it? Even I cannot believe such bold disobedience and disappointing behavior from you.

You have always been my favorite son. I have poured every effort into you, and I have plans for your future that you would never imagine. I know this will be hard for you to hear, but being in love with that girl is a mistake. A mistake that I will not let you make. You may not understand right now, but you will. I do this only out of love for you, my heart. By the time this reaches you, I will have this servant girl safely out of your life. She will soon be married to another and you will never hear from her again.

Do not try to see her again or I will have to do something even more drastic. Try to focus on the things ahead - your grand graduation, for one.

Your proud mother,

Queen Lilian

His heartbeat pounded in his ears. He pressed fists to his eyes until he saw colors, trying to keep the hot tears back.

CHAPTER NINE

Present

After a week of kitchen duty, Joran was more than ready for a different task, even if it meant he and Peter would be working together. Maniv clucked his tongue at him when he stalked around the galley saying, "At least you're not emptying chamber pots," but cleaning fish and scrubbing greasy pots was close enough.

The sun was hot on deck. It wasn't any more comfortable out here than it was in the galley with a fire they had to hover near to keep an eye on so it didn't catch the ship on fire. Sweat dripped down his back, and he rolled his shoulders to get rid of the tickle. Peter was bent over thick ropes, patiently loosening knots, and working them into a neat coil.

Joran stretched. There was a shady corner on the other side of the deck and he eyed it carefully.

"I'll be back in a bit," he said casually, heading the opposite way, but planning to circle back to the shady spot. He hadn't been sleeping well recently. Maybe it was because his body still missed the drugs, but his dreams had been terrible. A nap would help. And he would shave off a few minutes of his time on duty instead of breaking his back over some dumb ropes.

He slumped down in the corner and let his eyelids sink shut. His mind started to sink as well, the warmth of the sun and the lull of the ship relaxing him immediately. A thud against his thigh woke him with a jolt.

Peter was staring down at him. "Get up. You're on duty."

"Curse the spirits, Peter, leave me alone. I'm not your child."

"Still my duty."

"No, seriously, it's not. Your duty is getting calluses from the spirits-blasted rope, not making sure that I'm doing the same. For a *servant*, you are stuck up."

Peter didn't flinch. "The Captain expects all of us to do our share. I'm trying to save your hide from getting in trouble," he rejoined calmly.

Joran was wide awake now and seething. Anger caused his words to rush out before he could stop them. "I've done my duty today, as much as I care to do. I don't give a hoot whether the ropes are neat and tidy or not. I don't care if this ship sails at all. I didn't choose to be here. If you remember, I was forced. My spirits-blasted father hated me so much, he had to get rid of me, so he sent me all the way to another kingdom and then beyond - to the sea." His voice had risen considerably, but Peter met his glare steadily.

"Joran, maybe your father doesn't hate you. Maybe he cares."

The memory of his father's hand against his cheek burned in his mind. "You don't understand. You're living every kid's dream job before you even leave your teen years, probably because you have rich parents who pay your way into everything you want."

Peter drew his brows together in surprise. "Is that what you think?"

"What else should I think? Please don't try to tell me that you had it hard too. What, you're a poor orphan whose parents died, who had to scrabble his way to the top?" Joran scoffed.

"Yes, actually," Peter murmured. His expression was still stolid.

Joran's face was on fire, but the sun had nothing to do with it. He hated being here. He hated that Peter could never be shaken. It always made him try harder, which left him feeling like a horrible person in the end. Like now. Spirits, he hated that Peter had lost someone to death, but even more, he hated how calmly he handled the fact being thrown at him. Joran hated that he felt irritable every minute of the day. It made him lash out, and the more he did it, the worse he felt.

He just didn't know how to stop.

He gestured to Peter with a crude symbol that he certainly hadn't learned at the castle and stalked away.

CHAPTER TEN

One Year Ago

Joran left the Academy immediately. He grabbed only the necessities and hurried out to prepare his horse. He wouldn't be able to get permission, he was sure, even if he had time. He would be in trouble for this. He may even risk his enrollment, but he had left a note saying it was an emergency, and he hoped the Commander would look at it and find mercy in his heart.

He rode hard, stopping only when he had to rest and refresh his horse. He even hired a fresh horse in one of the towns, leaving his own to be cared for until he returned.

He was exhausted when he reached Lady Marty's home in Glensprit. She was a single lady, who lived in a sensible home near the city. The grounds weren't extensive because she preferred practicality. He dismounted in the town, leaving his horse at an inn's stable to be cared for. His legs were stiff, and he was sore, but he didn't even stop to eat before hiring a coach to take him to the address on the edge of town.

***

Joran smiled at Krynn's mother. She had large, blue eyes like Krynn's, and her hair fell in the same pleated waves, but it was a soft-iron gray.

"I'll protect her, I promise," he vowed.

She nodded through pinched brows. "I know, Your Highness. I don't want to lose her – to this other man, or to you, but you've proven yourself. You've risked much for her already. She's told me everything, and we – I – trust you. How it happened that a prince fell in love with my daughter, I'll never know, but I thank the One that it's true, and I know she is worthy of you."

"It is I that am not worthy of her," he said sincerely.

"Please take care of her. Find a way to tell me everything as soon as you can."

Krynn hugged her mother, then took Joran's hand. Together, they crept into the moonlight.

Later, Joran would wish he had just taken her to a magister who could marry them right then, but he hadn't. He had cradled her in his arms in the saddle as they rode by moonlight to the castle in Lilt.

CHAPTER ELEVEN

Present

Joran stood alone, staring at the inky water. The darkness settled around him like a cloak. He gripped the railing, the salty moisture that had gathered there stinging his blisters. Blast the salt. It made his clothes dry stiff after they were washed, and it coated his hair and skin, making him feel sticky.

He wasn't in the mood to join the nightly gathering below decks, but he also wasn't in the mood to speak to Captain Markus when he walked up.

They stood silently for a few minutes before the Captain spoke. "The sea is different at night. All these years, and I still feel I don't know her in the darkness." He paused. "I feel a storm behind us. I think we'll outrun it, but we still need to be prepared. Which reminds me, I've heard that you've been slacking on your duties."

Joran shrugged, his energy to volley completely gone.

"We're a team, Joran. The members of the Pearl work together, for each other. I don't tolerate laziness."

"What about members who don't want to be on the Pearl?" Joran shot back, though his tone lacked fire.

Captain Markus regarded him, his sharp eyes seeming to see inside him, even in the dark.

"I know you don't want to be here, Joran, but that doesn't change the fact that you are. Your father thought –"

"My father didn't think for years, and when he finally did, he thought wrong." Bitterness laced the words.

Captain Markus sighed. "Everything happened so quickly. It couldn't have been easy for any of you. I only got the briefest statement of events in the message saying you were coming. I'm convinced King Henry loves you and sent you here in what he believed was your best interest."

A bitter snort escaped. Joran pressed his fingers to his forehead, his turbulent feelings threatening to overtake him.

"Do you know why I named my ship the Pearl?"

Of course not. Joran shook his head.

"What do you know about pearls?"

Joran sighed. What was the Captain getting at? "They're found in the water. They're somewhat valuable, women wear them as jewelry."

"Hmm, yes. A pearl is formed inside an oyster. Whenever a bit of shell or something harsh lodges inside the oyster, it creates a substance to cover it. Eventually, after many layers of the substance hardens over the foreign object, it no longer causes the oyster discomfort. In fact, it has become a thing of beauty."

The muscles in Joran's jaw twitched. Memories of pain were crashing through his mind. The way his father ignored him. The night he lost Krynn. The guilt for the things he'd done. His father's slap. Being sent away.

Captain Markus laid a hand on his shoulder. Joran stiffened but didn't shake him off.

"Black pearls are extremely rare. I heard the Great Magister revoked all magic from gems and crystals, but legend was that black pearls could fix anything that was broken."

Joran narrowed his eyes. A broken heart? Nothing could fix that. Besides, the Captain was right. The Great Magister Erlich, the keeper of all the magic in Kerrynth, had revealed himself during the revolt, after years of living in hiding. Saddened by the greed of Queen Lilian and worried about future evil intentions

Of Oceans and Pearls

from others, he had revoked all power from crystals, leaving no magic but individual gifts the One bestowed on certain people. Pearls would do nothing for him now.

Captain Markus spoke again, bringing his thoughts back to the present. "I prefer to appreciate them simply for what they are – beautiful. What starts as something irritating and painful becomes something lustrous and strong. Especially black pearls. They remind me that the darkest nights, the layers of suffering and pain, meld together in the end to shine."

Joran hunched his shoulders, and Captain Markus let his hand drop.

"So beauty comes from brokenness?" Joran's voice sounded brittle over the waves.

Captain Markus lifted his shoulders. "It can. Pain changes you, that much is sure. Whether you let it destroy you or make you shine, that's up to you." He raised his face to the black sky. "Pearls aren't the only example of that, you know. Some say even the stars are on fire, but just look at how they adorn the night."

When he shifted away, Joran chanced a glance at the sky. Millions of stars glittered in the vast dome.

He brushed at the salty moisture gathered on his cheeks only to realize that it hadn't come from sea spray, but from tears.

CHAPTER TWELVE

One year ago

The powdery, jasmine scent of Krynn's hair filled Joran's senses as he encircled her in the saddle.

"It will be okay," he promised in her ear, leaning closer to nuzzle her neck.

She leaned back, resting her head against his shoulder.

"You came, Joran. It's already okay."

He grinned and squeezed her before growing serious again. "I will explain to my mother. She has always said she would do anything to make me happy, and you make me happy, Krynn. We'll make her see that. I'll tell her I'm planning to marry you."

She turned her face so her lips met his. Warmth spread through his core when her soft lips brushed his, and he loosened the reins on the horse letting him trot along, while tightening his arms around Krynn and drawing her even closer.

***

"What is this?" Queen Lilian was as close to screeching as Joran had ever heard her.

He and Krynn had arrived at the castle after a day and a half of riding. The Queen was gaping at them now.

Joran kept Krynn's small hand in his. Already, his mother's eyes had narrowed and his gut clenched.

"Mother," he bowed respectfully. "This –"

"What are you doing here, Joran? Do you have approved leave from the Academy? Why is she here?" She spit the questions at him, her lip curling at Krynn.

He gripped Krynn's hand tighter. "Is Father here? I need to speak to both of you. *We* need to speak to you. This is Krynn Astrior."

Queen Lilian's nostrils flared.

"Get her out of the castle, Joran. Now. I never want to see her again or hear you speak her name." Her tone bubbled with rage.

"You don't understand—"

"*You* don't understand, Joran. You don't understand anything," she shrieked. She grabbed his shirtfront and pulled.

He arched back, surprised. He had expected his mother to be unhappy, but he had never seen her so outraged.

He could feel Krynn trembling.

Queen Lilian stepped toward him, her face close to his. "How could you disregard my instructions like this? You are going to be king, Joran. I will make you *king*. That has always been my plan for you. Do not ruin it." She hissed each word.

Joran's jaw dropped.

She wanted him to be king? Benrid was the older twin. He was the heir to the throne. Why? How would she do it?

Queen Lilian threw a withering glance at Krynn. "Be gone with you, and don't ever come back, or I'll have the guards after you."

Krynn's face was white. She faltered, glancing from Joran to the Queen. Her hand slipped out of his, and he clenched his empty fist, but didn't try to grab her back.

He didn't know what to do. If the Queen brought in the guards, who knew what she would decree for Krynn? Banishment, imprisonment?

Krynn stumbled back, tears making her eyes glassy.

Joran took a step after her. He couldn't just let her leave.

Queen Lilian locked her fingers around his arm. "If you follow, she will die."

He froze.

Panic made him dizzy. This wasn't how it was supposed to go. Krynn was being forced away, and he couldn't follow. Surely she knew he would find her as soon as he could, didn't she? His mother was in a rage. Father? Perhaps the King would help him.

Krynn was shaking as she backed away, finally turning and stumbling down the long hall.

"Krynn, I love you. I'll find you," Joran called, desperate to let her know, despite his mother's threats.

***

Joran found his father in the courtroom. Court was already in session for the day, but he sent a servant with an urgent message saying he needed to see him immediately. He watched as the King read the message, then glanced around the room, finally locating his son. He nodded imperceptibly, and Joran could finally take a full breath as relief seeped in. A few minutes later, the King excused himself.

Joran's guards had been summoned. They didn't accompany him at the Academy, but they would be glued to his side now, especially since he had made the trip alone, without any kind of protection. They followed him as he left the courtroom to meet his father in the back hall.

To his dismay, the Queen was already there when he spotted his father coming from the back entrance of the courtroom. She glided up to the King, rested her hand on his arm for a moment, and then left the room. Joran squinted after her, but she never turned around.

"Your Majesty," he greeted his father formally. "I made a desperate, sudden departure from the Academy because of an emergency. I'm here to procure your help," he started in a rush. He was about to launch into his story when he noticed the King's unfocused eyes.

"It is so nice to see you, Son. I trust your studies are going well." The King smiled in adoration.

"Yes, Father, but I need you to help me convince Mother of something. There is a girl I met eight years ago. We've been –"

"Mother, of course. You can dine with us tonight. She will be so happy to see you."

Joran pulled his eyebrows together in confusion.

"I want to marry this girl," he cut to the point.

"I must get back to court now," the King said kindly. "It was wonderful to catch up with you. You were gone too long." Then he turned and walked away.

Joran gawked at his father's back. He was speechless. His father had been aloof many times, but this was a record. He acted as though he hadn't heard a word Joran had said.

Footsteps sounded behind him, clicking smartly over the tiles. A servant handed him a message. Joran unfolded the small paper. It was from the Queen.

***

Joran hurried to the Queen's quarters. Her note said she had overreacted, but was ready to talk it over with him now.

The long days of riding had left him exhausted, and every step he took felt bruised. He needed to bathe and get into fresh clothes. He rubbed his forehead, trying to clear his thoughts, which were clouded with fatigue. None of it mattered. All that mattered was that he could be with Krynn.

"Come in, Son, sit with me," The Queen invited from her sitting room.

Joran sat stiffly on the edge of the sofa. The long seat cushion was covered in red silk and adorned with matching pillows, but he didn't lean into them.

Queen Lilian smiled from her chair opposite him, her arms resting languidly on the sides. "You surprised me, you know. You can't do that to your mother – look how I reacted."

"Where's Krynn?" he asked, still terse.

"Oh, I don't know where she went, but the guards confirmed she left through the gates, so at least she's obedient."

His jaw tightened.

"Here's the thing, Joran," his mother continued easily, her green eyes unusually bright. "If you really want this girl, we can make it work. Obviously you cannot marry a commoner, but I do believe I could find a way to get her adopted by a noble family, so at least she would have their name. Then it wouldn't be a disgrace, and you could both be happy."

Joran's eyebrows shot up in surprise. "Really?"

"Of course." She leaned forward, letting her eyes linger on his, and a distracting buzzing filled his mind. He felt it more than heard it. "Anything to see my son happy. I can still make you king, if you work with me. It will be our secret. Now, go find her and bring her to me."

***

Joran tore out of the castle gates, frantic and ecstatic at the same time. He shook his head, trying to clear the fog, which had settled deeper in his mind since his talk with his mother. Krynn. She had said to find Krynn. She was going to make him king. He had to bring Krynn back.

He found Krynn easily enough at an inn. Her face was tear-soaked, and she hadn't taken the pain to change or freshen up either, but he didn't care. He whooped and grabbed her hands, twirling with her right between the tables.

"I knew it would be all right," he said.

"What happened?" She gave him a cautious smile, her expression hopeful.

He suddenly couldn't remember why he was there. What was he supposed to be doing? He tilted his head, searching Krynn's face for answers. She was so pretty. He smiled and shook his head, unconcerned with the fog in his brain. "Mother said to find you," he said simply.

***

After a meal and a good night's sleep, Joran woke up feeling like the day before had been a hazy dream. He could barely piece together the events, but he didn't care to try. Krynn was here, his mother was helping them, and soon he would marry his best friend.

"I've arranged everything. She sails down to Terind in two days," Queen Lilian told him at dinner. "King Henry sent a message to the Academy asking them to excuse your hurried exit and to expect you back at the end of the week."

He and Krynn wandered outside. "The lake?" he asked, smiling.

"Of course," she grinned back.

He waved his guards away, wanting privacy.

They strolled along the water for a while. "I'm scared to sail to meet the Harins by myself," Krynn admitted.

He squeezed her fingers, which were nestled in his.

"My mother will understand, I'm sure," she went on, "But you don't think this will mean I can never see her again, do you?"

"Of course not. I believe the Harins are only extending their old family name to you as a favor to the Kingdom, rather than expecting you to act as a real daughter."

"I'm grateful. I've never been on a boat before, though."

"It will be a short trip. You'll be fine. While you head to Terind to change your name, I'll head back to the Academy to finish up there, and in three months, we'll be together again. Mother says she will start planning and the wedding can happen as soon as I return."

Krynn let out a happy sigh, and he bumped into her playfully.

She pushed him back, and he pretended to stagger a step to the side before returning the blow.

"Hey," she squealed, stumbling this time. She ran at him, and he darted off, laughing.

He let her chase him for a while, then turned suddenly and caught her as she plowed into his arms. He tripped back a step and lost his footing, sending them both sprawling onto the grass.

They laughed as they fell. Joran lay on his back in the long grass, breathing in the scent of wet earth and jasmine. Krynn rolled over to lie beside him, the movement sliding her hair off his face. She snuggled into the crook of his shoulder, sighing contentedly. He pulled her tightly against him with his arm. Her fingers ran lightly over his chest, drawing circles on his shirt until he caught them with his other hand, bringing them to his mouth and kissing her fingertips.

Please don't ever let this end, he prayed.

***

Of Oceans and Pearls

Joran rode in the carriage with Krynn to the river the morning she was to set sail. His mother had allowed them a royal carriage, the shiny black paint an icon in the city, even without the silver crest. Although his guard sat on top with the driver, they were alone inside. He pulled the gray curtains closed.

"Kiss me, Birdie," he whispered, thankful for the closed top of the carriage.

She giggled and turned her face to him. He pulled at her lips greedily, desire coursing through him when she moaned. His tongue ran over her bottom lip and darted into her mouth. She opened for him, welcoming him, and he was lost.

"Krynn," he murmured her name moments later against the soft skin of her neck. Finally, he slid from the bench seat to his knees on the floor.

He pulled a small, golden ring from his pocket. It was engraved with leafy trailing details, and it reminded him so much of her fairy-like self that he had bought it as soon as he had seen it.

"Will you marry me, my love?"

A sudden bump on the road sent his chin into her knee, and she pealed with laughter. He righted himself and grinned sheepishly.

She leaned forward and slid her fingers into his light hair. "That is the one and only thing I long to do, my prince."

He took her hand, gently sliding the ring down her finger.

"The little bird has become a princess," he whispered.

CHAPTER THIRTEEN

Present

Joran stayed at the rails for a long time after the Captain's talk, letting the tears slide down his face and the wind blow them dry. The midnight watch had switched with the former lookout before he finally descended the stairs to his hammock.

***

He waited until Krynn's boat had set sail and was out of sight before he left. She had stood on the deck waving and watching him for a long time. She had even blown him a kiss, the sunlight glinting off her new ring. Joran grinned as he started his journey back to the Academy, his guards taking their positions behind him to escort him back. He would still have to face the wrath of the Commander when he got back, but knowing he was one step closer to being with Krynn would make anything bearable.

His father's message must have smoothed everything over with the Commander, who welcomed him sternly, but did not reprimand him for running away. Benrid, on the other hand, glared at him suspiciously. Joran would have some explaining to do later.

"You resume your studies in the morning and will have to remain later in the training yard to make up for the past week of missed maneuvers. Your graduation is just around the corner," the Commander clipped.

He nodded smartly, unconcerned. Life looked brighter than it ever had, and he was eager to face it head on.

Except he did not resume classes in the morning.

The morning post brought a message. It had been sent the day after Joran had left and was in his mother's own hand.

"My deepest regrets, Son, but there has been a tragedy. The ship Miss Astrior left on was attacked by river pirates the evening after they set sail. The ship was raided, and the girl was murdered. An investigation has already begun."

His heart stopped. Time stopped. He sank to the floor, trembling. Hours passed, though he wasn't aware of it. Eventually his room grew dark. It was Benrid who was sent to find him that evening.

"Brother?" Benrid's long face scrunched in concern.

Joran jerked toward the voice, as if waking out of a nightmare. Benrid crossed the room and crouched beside him. He noticed the paper on the floor and picked it up, holding it close to his face to make out the words in the waning light.

Of Oceans and Pearls

Even in the shadows, Joran saw his brother's face pale and he looked at Joran in horror.

"It was her, wasn't it? The girl you always write to?"

He waited, but Joran couldn't move. Couldn't answer.

Benrid had never been his friend, but for once, he acted like a brother. He put his hand on Joran's shoulder and squeezed.

"I think you should return. If there is a remembrance ceremony, you should be there. I'll speak to the Commander."

True to his word, Benrid had Joran on his way back to Lilt just a few hours later. A carriage had been provided this time, and he dozed off and on as they traveled through the night.

He hadn't spoken to anyone. He wasn't sure he remembered how to talk anymore. Nothing seemed real. Time didn't exist. It was as if everything was blank and dark, even inside his mind.

His mother didn't seem surprised to see him back, though he read annoyance in her features.

"Well, you're here in time to see her. The body was being prepared for transport. We're sending her back to her mother in the morning. That woman and Lady Marty can decide on the burial and remembrance. She's no longer our responsibility."

The coarse words grated against his heart, but all he said was, "Where is she?"

Nothing could have prepared him for the agony.

Of Oceans and Pearls

Krynn was in a wooden crate, stretched out like she was sleeping. She wore the same dress she had on when she boarded the river boat, now though, it was torn and stained with blood from her chest to her legs. Apparently she was not even good enough to warrant a change of clothes in death. The dried blood had turned the pale creamy fabric a dull brown. She'd bled. So much. Pain washed over him like he was feeling it with her. She had been stabbed through the heart. The mortician had straightened her face and limbs, but she looked unnatural and stiff. The pale swollen face on the pillow wasn't like his Krynn, his birdie, with gentle features.

His lips trembled as he whispered. "Krynn. You must have been terrified, my love."

Hot tears filled his eyes for the first time since he'd received the news, burning his chest and throat as they flooded him. A raw sound erupted from within him, echoing against the stone walls as his heart broke. He touched his finger to her lips, the lips he had teased and kissed just a few mornings ago. They were stiff. He shuddered.

Then his eyes fell on something else. Her left hand lay beside her, near her wrist, but oddly distant. It was detached, like it had been sawn off, the bone visible. The stumps had been rubbed with an orange oil to preserve them, making the raw flesh glow sickeningly, even with the blood washed away. Her fingers were gray, the gold band he had given her appeared garish against her stony skin.

He fell to his knees and retched on the tiles.

His mother came in with men, curling her lips at the vomit. "Really, Joran." She motioned to the men, who closed the crate.

Joran came alive. He flew to his feet, lashing out at them. They couldn't take her away from him. Not again. He held onto the crate, pulling against the four men who tried to lift it.

"No!" he screamed. "You can't take her. I'll never leave her again."

Queen Lilian sighed. "Guards, restrain him."

They pulled him from behind. He swung his arms blindly, but strong hands caught his arms and held them fast. Sobs tore through him as Krynn was carried out of sight. He didn't have the strength to fight.

His legs buckled and the guards released him. Everyone left and the door closed after them. Joran was in a heap on the floor, sobs shredding him from the inside. He cried until his strength was gone. He couldn't even move.

He wanted to die.

***

Joran jerked awake, sending his hammock swinging wildly. He gasped into the darkness, but was met with the usual, steady snores. He touched his face. It was soaked with tears.

He pressed his palm against his mouth, Krynn's ring pressed into his lips. Her mother had sent it back to him. It was all he had of her.

The dream had faded when he opened his eyes, but the memory – he would remember forever. He tried not to let his sobs escape, but the scalding tears chased each other down his cheeks. Before tonight, he hadn't cried for a long time. He had returned to the Academy to finish his last few weeks of training, feeling like an empty shell of himself. He did his work quietly, even though he often lost his train of thought. His marks fell, and when graduation came, he was in sixth place in the special honors, two places behind Benrid. It didn't matter.

He didn't process his sadness once he was home either. There was no one to grieve with him. His mother was relieved Krynn was out of the way, promising that she would find someone better for him. In fact, she nearly insinuated that she'd wanted Krynn to die. He resented her. His father assured him there was an investigation going on, but nothing ever came of it, and the King never once offered a word of sympathy or comfort. Joran wasn't sure Golan, the youngest of the three brothers, was even aware of what had happened. Benrid was kinder than usual, but that summer he went unexplainably blind, and when he lost his eyesight, he fell into his own pit of despair. Queen Lililan locked Benrid safely away to hide his sudden anomaly, while the King pondered whether he should remove the appointment to the throne from his eldest son. It seemed everyone lived in their own turmoil, strangers existing in the same household.

Meanwhile, Joran didn't want to be alive any longer, but he lived. The world went on, sunrises and sunsets following each other. He was desperate to distract himself. One night he snuck out. He got drunk for the first time that night and he liked it. It made him forget for a while. Later he discovered that drugs were an even better escape. He liked the abandon of gambling too, the rush of freedom he felt. He started street fighting a few months later. He embraced the pain in his bones from the punches and let the pain in his heart seep into his own throws. He enjoyed other girls. He took advantage of them, savoring the moment of power he felt when he was with them, so different from his own helplessness to save Krynn. None of it lasted, but it helped him get by.

He sniffed.

Peter's hammock shifted, bumping gently into his own.

"Who is it you miss?"

Peter's voice startled him. He held his breath, considering not answering.

"Someone broke your heart."

It was a simple statement, but it pierced him.

"She died." He whispered.

"What was her name?"

"Krynn." Her name hung in the air, in the blackness. He hadn't said it for so long. The syllable brought a rush of images to his mind – her pleated curls, her long dresses, her deft fingers twisting in his hair. "I was going to marry her. I met her when I was 10 and we became friends. We saw each other every year at my birthday celebration festival and we fell in love. She loved birds. And animals. She would never watch the archery competitions because she hated seeing the hogs die."

A smile touched his lips. He had never told anyone those things.

Peter was silent. Joran couldn't see his face, but he could feel him waiting.

"She loved nature. I gave her the ring I wear because of the vines and leaves on it. It was so much like her. My mother didn't want us to marry because she wasn't noble-blooded. She decided Krynn had to take the name of an old noble line for us to marry. Krynn was to sail to Terind to change her name, but she never made it. She was murdered by river pirates." His voice cracked.

"That's why you have bad dreams." Joran wasn't sure if it was a statement or a question.

Joran rubbed his forehead. "I have a lot of nightmares, but the worst are about her...her dying, yes."

He took a breath, surprised that his tears had stopped. Saying everything out loud, letting the words fill the dark space above him, loosened something tight inside.

"I'm sorry, Joran," Peter's voice was low and genuine. "I know you wish you could have saved her, but all you can do now is to let your life honor her."

Joran exhaled. The way he had used innocent girls, drank until he passed out, and stolen from the treasury to buy drugs – his past year of recklessness swam in his vision.

"I – I can't," he choked.

"You can start now. An honorable life will honor her existence. She influenced you and made you who you are today. If you strive to be a good person, you honor her by your actions."

Joran was silent, letting the words sink in.

Peter shifted again. It felt like he was sitting up straighter. "What are your parents like?" he asked.

Joran cocked his head and glanced toward his guard, even though he could barely make him out in the darkness. No one had been interested in his life since Krynn.

"My mother was executed just before I was sent away." Words tumbled out, the whole story falling out of his mouth without hesitation. He wanted to stop talking, but he didn't.

Peter listened to his stories about the Queen's power to control minds, and the way Joran had finally realized what she was doing. She'd used the stolen power on him many times before he caught on. Not long before the revolt, she had even tried to force him into marrying a magically gifted girl, Princess Avalon from Haven. Even though he'd gotten better at avoiding looking into the Queen's eyes which was the way she could transfer her control, sometimes she still tricked him into meeting her gaze. Other times, he'd been too carried away by the drugs to care.

"Thank the One, that manipulated marriage didn't actually go through – although it was Golan and the Great Magister who intervened."

Peter didn't comment, but listened as Joran told him about the way his father succumbed to the Queen's power, about his brother's struggles, and his own dip into a baser life.

He could feel dawn coming on, even though no light had seeped over the horizon yet. His eyelids were heavy, and he trailed off. He slept soundly until sunrise.

CHAPTER FOURTEEN

Peter shook him by the shoulder. Joran dragged himself out of sleep, opening his eyes to focus on Peter. Memories of the night flooded back, and he felt a flush warm his neck. Spirits. He had told Peter about her. About everything. He had cried.

He sat up quickly, avoiding his guard's eyes. The other swinging beds were empty. Light filtered down the stairs. He would be late for breakfast if he didn't hurry.

He pulled his nightshirt off and replaced it with a stiff, salt-water-washed one, his back to Peter. How was he supposed to act? He felt like Peter could see right through him now, and he loathed the feeling. Things were going to be awkward.

"Didn't want you to miss breakfast," Peter's voice commented behind him. "I'm mending sails today, so I'm off."

With that, Peter strode up the stairs to the deck. Joran shot a glance after him, grateful that he hadn't mentioned last night's conversation.

***

Joran learned he was also mending sails. Tips, the older sailor who demonstrated for them, worked in serious silence, his bushy brows twisted together over his work.

Peter sat with his normal, calm demeanor, the thread and needle obeying his deft fingers easily. Joran fought a scowl as he struggled with the flimsy objects. The breeze tugged at his string, making it hard not to tangle. At least Peter wasn't going to talk about Joran bearing his heart last night.

He didn't want it brought up, and he didn't want to continue the conversation. He snuck a glance at the guard. Spirits, so young. Peter had a dip in his bottom lip and shapely black brows. He'd make a pretty girl happy one day. Joran looked away, embarrassed by the things he suddenly felt.

Even if he didn't plan on speaking civilly to Peter again, he was grateful that he had listened last night.

***

They had been sailing close enough to land that it was visible every now and then, but Joran was surprised when instead of sailing along the coast, the ship changed course and headed straight for the hazy shore in the distance. He heard two sailors talking about a town and realized they were making a stop. He felt excitement rise. He was ready to get off this creaky ship and explore a new place.

The wind was favorable and carried them quickly toward shore. The Captain maneuvered the ship carefully, checking the depth often to make sure they didn't run aground. When he was satisfied, they furled the sails and began rotating the capstan to let down the anchor. Joran stood back as the crew worked, unsure of the new routine, but he quickly fell in with the group of sailors who lined up to disembark over the side once the longboat was lowered. Peter was below decks and Joran hoped he could get onto land and disappear into the crowds before his guard could follow.

He turned as he felt a hand on his shoulder. Kirk pulled him back a step. "Captain doesn't want you to leave this time around," he said.

Joran frowned. The first mate was a decent man, but at this moment, he wanted to punch him. "What do you mean, I can't leave?"

Captain Markus himself suddenly appeared. "That's right, Joran. Not at this port. You haven't been pulling your share of the load and I honestly don't know if I can trust you out of my sight yet."

Irritation flared. "Not pulling my share of the load? I work my backside off every day for you ungrateful people." He held up his blistered hands. "I'm the bloody Prince, and this isn't an official prison, much as you try to make it seem like one."

He turned to stalk over the side of the ship, only to find Peter standing in his way. He groaned.

"Have you ever seen one of these?" The Captain's question made him glance back.

Captain Markus swung a short, curved sword. The blade got wider at the tip, which was tapered from a sharp point to a curve. Joran watched the unusual weapon spin in the air.

"A friend gave me a pair of these when I visited the earth kingdoms once. They're unique to his country. They're often used in pairs, but I could never master the dual swing, although I'm decent with one. I cannot allow you to leave the ship, but perhaps this will help you pass the time here. Would you like to try?"

Joran didn't want to agree, but curiosity got the best of him. He had never held a sword like that, but he had been good with his longsword. Besides, with even his daggers confiscated when he boarded the ship, it had been too long since he'd felt the heft of a weapon in his hands, grounding him.

He shrugged, catching the sword the Captain tossed to him. They squared off, the Captain advancing first. The blade was lighter, easier to flick than the longsword he had trained with, but he wasn't used to the proximity. He squinted in concentration as he met the Captain's blows.

Captain Markus halted the round after he had scored five hits to Joran's one. Joran was breathing hard, but he could feel himself smiling. He stretched his neck from side to side, trying to hide his good mood.

The Captain nodded to the curved sword Joran held. "I think you should keep that. You're not bad with it."

Joran looked at him in surprise.

"I have matters to attend to. Care to practice?" The Captain addressed Peter this time, who sat to the side, sketching on paper balanced on his knee.

Peter looked up, folded the drawing and put it in his pocket along with his pencil. He took the second sword, resting the blade against his other palm as he turned it, getting a feel for the weight.

Joran stuttered a thank you to the Captain as he left and turned to Peter with a mischievous smirk. He pulled his shirt over his head, already slightly sweating. He rolled his shoulders back, then flexed. "Hmm, sure you don't want to do the same? This range of motion might give me an advantage."

Peter smiled and smoothed his dark shirt. "I rather appreciate formality, actually."

Joran snorted.

"And I think you may need the advantage," Peter grinned.

They fenced for over an hour.

When they finally finished the last round, Joran leaned back against the railing, drawing deep breaths. Peter was surprisingly good. He'd had excellent training somewhere, and he adjusted to the new weapon quickly. Joran studied the strange swooping blade in his own hand. He liked it.

He caught Peter staring at his chest.

His tattoo. He'd forgotten. His eyes dropped to where small wings were inked above his heart. No one except the man who had drawn it there knew about it. He'd had it done one night when he'd had just enough ale to make him impetuous. It reminded him of Krynn, his little bird. Wings. Perhaps she really had them now in the afterlife.

"It's her. I like it," Peter said quietly, dropping his eyes.

Joran felt touched and defensive at the same time, which left him at a loss for words. He sauntered over to his shirt and pulled it back over his head.

CHAPTER FIFTEEN

While they had hugged the coast of Terind in the beginning, Captain Markus had ventured much further from the mainland since their first port. Although Joran hadn't left the ship that time, he'd gotten his fill of news from the others when they got back. Apparently, the liberation of the gifted people, the ones who had been born with magical abilities, was causing ripple effects all through Kerrynth. Even the Kingdom of Haven, who wasn't closely allied with any of the other kingdoms in Kerrynth and had always boasted itself to be void of magic, had to reevaluate their stance with the news that their very own princess, Avalon, was gifted. Johnny laughed when he said it, as though it were a joke, but Joran remained serious for once. He had almost married Princess Avalon, when his mother had orchestrated it and had him and Avalon under her control. Then later, he tried to kill Avalon. He wondered how her newly found abilities were impacting her kingdom.

Kirk, who tended to see things in a serious light, pursed his lips and added, "The tremors of unrest are dangerous. I spent one day in the town and heard talk from both ends. Some say it's a blessing to have the magic back, others are afraid and say it's a curse."

"Of course everyone has an opinion," Serb said. "What's the danger in that?"

"People will go to great lengths to protect themselves from things they fear. Someone told me there was a public flogging here last week. A gifted man was trying to perform magic - water shaping or some such thing - for an audience, trying to make some coin. He was caught and beaten and told never to return."

Serb nodded, conceding.

Later, the Captain himself addressed them all. "Men, our patrol is extending now, due to the events in Kerrynth. The magical crystals, while legally banned, used to bring in a profit on the black market. Now that the rocks are powerless, smugglers are looking for new ways to profit. Authorities warned me that many have set their sights beyond our kingdoms. There are already reports of pirates raiding at sea."

Eyebrows raised, Joran's included.

"Although it has only been a few weeks, other black market items have been springing up. Gems from other lands seem to be in demand, probably with the hope that they have some kind of power the way ours used to. But worst of all, it seems the drug trade is flourishing, financed in part from the royal treasury itself."

Shock rippled through the group.

"Apparently the former queen had quite an interest in the business herself and worked closely with a supplier named Felix Bagden. The King and his council are only now discovering their own laws and decisions were tainted with her deception, seeing as how they were supporting Bagden."

Joran thought of his mother's mind control, his jaw clenching. He'd always assumed she had used it mostly on her family, perhaps on some servants. She had been evil, but perhaps he hadn't even known the extent. She must have been using her power on the council members too. His mind sped up. If she were responsible for the spread of drugs in Kerrynth, he had supported her schemes by becoming a buyer. He felt sick.

The Captain was still talking. "King Henry is working to undo the policies, but it's a bit like stopping a rolling snowball at this point. It will take time."

"Are we after Felix Bagden, then?" someone questioned.

"Not specifically. His band is too widespread for us alone. However, any information you glean would be helpful. I'm just letting you all know what I've learned. We will be heading further out to sea, though, watching for those who are raiding merchant ships as well as jewel smugglers."

"Has selling foreign jewels in Kerrynth become illegal?" Joran spoke up.

"Only if they were acquired by ill means. There hasn't been time for the proper trade contracts to be established, which means most of the jewels have been stolen from other lands. Then they're smuggled into Kerrynth without passing the inspections or paying import taxes."

With that sobering news, the Pearl's bow eased south as they sailed further into the Bristian Ocean. Life fell into a routine. Joran walked easily across the rolling ship now. He worked during the day, laughed with the men in the evenings, and slept better at night. He'd gotten used to the film of salt on his skin and hair. Two months had passed since he had first boarded the Pearl.

He and Peter were civil to each other, but Joran kept his distance. He still spotted the young man praying in the mornings. Somehow, his guard was always awake before him, usually ready for the day before Joran even opened his eyes.

This morning he watched him as he kneeled. *I wonder who he prays for?* The question crossed his mind. He didn't really know anything about Peter. Did he have siblings? A girl? Peter shifted, and Joran looked away quickly so he wouldn't be caught staring. Something inside told him he should try to get to know him better, but he pushed the thought away.

The way Peter always prayed, the way he was unfailingly punctual and unruffled still bothered Joran. Sudden irritation flared. He wasn't sure if it was because of Peter or the fact that he was on kitchen duty again this week, but he had to let it out.

"Do the spirits hear you?" he asked, bitterness edging into his voice. He'd stopped thinking about the One a long time ago, though he didn't go so far as to blaspheme Him. He also didn't believe in the multi-faceted spirit religion popular in the Earth Kingdoms. He was pretty sure Peter didn't either, but he prodded just to get under his skin.

Peter raised his eyebrows. "I pray to the One. Yes, He hears."

"And yet your parents are dead," Joran stood, hating the words that came out, but unable to stop them.

Peter stilled. "It would make you feel better if I reacted, wouldn't it?" He gave a tight smile. "I won't get angry, Joran."

Joran clenched his jaw. *We'll see about that.*

***

Joran joined the men around the tables that evening. He still wasn't allowed to drink, but it didn't bother him as much as before. The crew treated him like one of them now, and sharing tall tales and teasing each other felt good.

"Captain told me more about why he changed the usual route," Kirk informed no one in particular. "He said he got a tip about that pirate assassin. He could be on these waters."

Something in his statement brought Joran's mind into sharp focus.

"The Left-Handed?" Pillow's eyes were wide.

Serb nodded. "That would be him. He's been on the loose for years. He used to travel the river, but word is that he's got a ship and taken to the seas now. Widening his horizons, most likely."

Joran heard a ringing in his ears and he felt cold. Peter glanced at him.

"The left-handed assassin? Who is he?" he demanded.

Johnny leaned forward, his elbows on the table. "He's mainly a raider, but he'll murder targets for the right price. He is missing his left hand, although he wears a false one, so it's not as easy an ailment to spot as you'd think."

Kirk frowned. "His signature mark is to cut off the left hand of his victim," he added. "He's known as the Left-Handed for obvious reasons. No one knows his real identity."

Joran's hands shook. Krynn. Her hand. He squeezed his eyes shut against the image. He had always suspected his mother had something to do with the bizarre death, but nothing to prove it. But if Krynn had been killed by an assassin…

"We're after him?" Joran asked.

Serb nodded. "That's what the Captain told Kirk." He glanced at the first mate for confirmation.

Joran growled, grabbing a mug of ale and gulping before anyone could stop him. If he ever met the man who killed Krynn, he'd wring his neck.

***

Joran burrowed deep into his hammock to keep from being pitched out. The ship was rocking violently, tossing sailors around like plankton in the waves. Surprisingly, most of the men slept soundly. Joran wasn't sure he could sleep through his first storm at sea. Mainly because the dizzy, familiar headache had returned, and he was hoping it wouldn't get worse and reach his stomach this time. Also, he had to admit, his nerves were on edge. The ship listed much too far to the side just then. The old wood groaned loudly, sounding like the ship was splitting in two, and Joran peered up at the rafters, trying to make sure everything was still intact. Captain Markus had assured them it wasn't a dangerous storm. "We'll just be tossed about a bit, men. I'll take two extra hands on deck tonight, but everyone else should ride it out below."

He hoped the Captain was right.

A blinding flash of lightning poured through the cracks, illuminating the bunk room in garish light for a split second. Pillows snorted loudly in his sleep, lumbering onto his side.

The flash had given Joran a brief opportunity to glance at Peter, but even in that short time, he could see his guard's fingers curled tightly around the edge of his hammock, his eyes too large in his face.

Joran thought back to the night Peter had talked to him, making him discuss his past, which had somehow distracted him from the torment of keeping it inside.

He cleared his throat.

"Are you awake?" he ventured in the direction of Peter's hammock.

A slight grunt.

"Have you ever been through a storm at sea?"

Peter inhaled. "No."

Joran's jaw twitched. He wasn't sure what to say.

"Neither have I," he admitted. "I guess the fact that most of the sailors are sleeping through it should be reassuring. I can't understand how they do it without toppling out of these things, though." He smiled, hoping Peter could hear it in his tone.

"Is this your first time at sea?" Peter seemed glad to continue the conversation.

"It is. I lived by a lake, so I learned how to swim early, and we went rowing often, sometimes traveled by boat on the river, but I had never seen the sea before I boarded this ship."

"It's immense."

Joran didn't need the reminder right now. He could already imagine the waves opening and sucking the ship down in a heartbeat, leaving no trace of them. He swallowed, trying to ignore the way the rain drummed on the deck above.

"Joran, I can't swim," Peter said. Joran had never heard anything but calm confidence in his guard's voice. He didn't like the fear that lingered in his tone now.

"I'm an excellent swimmer. I could swim for both of us, though I'm sure we don't need to worry about it now. If we were in danger, the Captain would alert us."

Peter seemed to recover some of his grip. "I bet you also claim to be a humble person."

A chuckle bubbled up Joran's throat. "Of course. Extremely humble, intelligent, strong, handsome, and charming. Did I miss anything?"

Peter snorted softly.

"So, Peter, your first job as a royal guard took you to sea. You've never sailed before and you can't even swim. And then putting up with me – this can't be what you wanted. Why did you choose to become a guard, anyway?"

Peter fidgeted in the dark. Joran glanced sideways at him in another flash of lightning. He was sitting up, his knees drawn up, staring into the distance.

"My grandfather," he finally offered. "He is a Captain General in the army. I trained under him for two years. I guess you could say I owe everything to him."

"A General? What's his name?"

"Jos Rehara."

The name didn't sound familiar, although Joran was generally up to date on the military leaders in Ethereal. He shrugged. He hadn't exactly been keen on keeping up with anything for the past year, he realized.

"How old are you?"

"Eighteen."

"Your grandfather must be highly respected. I don't know anyone that became a royal guard at that age."

"Something like that. Thank you."

"Don't let it go to your head," Joran teased. "This place is only big enough for one extremely humble person."

Joran wasn't sure, but he thought the pounding of the rain had softened a little. He settled back a little.

"What happened to your parents?" He asked softly.

Peter didn't answer for a long time. The darkness was thick between them, and the wind continued to plunge the ship up and down. Rain drummed outside, but not as harshly as before.

"My mother ran away from home to marry my father, but I never met him. He left her before I was born. She remarried because she was too proud to return home after the way she had left. My stepfather..."

Joran heard him swallow, despite the storm.

"He was...abusive...to her. Me. She died when I was twelve. I ran away after that. It took me a year to find my grandfather. I was thirteen, and he hadn't known I existed. I've lived with him ever since. Until now."

It had been a long time since Joran had felt someone else's pain, but his chest ached now, and for once, it wasn't his own grief he felt.

"I'm sorry," he finally offered, though the words felt horribly inefficient.

"Thank you," Peter said sincerely.

They were quiet for a long time. The wind and rain felt gentle now, and the waves rocked the ship at nearly their normal speed. Joran's eyelids were falling shut when he heard Peter speak again, barely above a whisper.

"I had a sister. I couldn't save her. She drowned."

Joran's stomach rolled, and he kept his eyes shut, trying to keep the wave of sadness at bay. Peter, the perfectly controlled young man who never snapped back at Joran for his rudeness, was grieving for his little sister. Peter felt guilty for not saving her —guilty for something he couldn't help. It tortured Joran.

"It wasn't your fault," he said sharply.

"But I was helpless. I didn't know what to do. I was ten. She was six, just a baby, really. There was a pond, and…and, I tried to get help, but my mother had snuck out to go shopping before my stepfather woke up. He was in a drunken stupor. He couldn't wake up."

Joran scrubbed at his own face, hating the tears he heard in Peter's voice, hating the pain he carried with him.

"How did you go on?" he asked hoarsely.

"It wasn't easy, Joran, and it still isn't. I live with her memory every day. It tore my mother apart. After that, her health plummeted. From that point, until I found my grandfather, those were the hardest years of my life. I wouldn't want anyone to live through what I did."

"But you seem fine now. No one would know," Joran whispered, desperate.

"I'll always live with thoughts of Lia, Joran. Always. But if I let her memory tear me apart, I'm not honoring her. I'm letting her beautiful little life destroy me. I decided to remember her for who she was – sweet, innocent, happy. I keep the beautiful memories wrapped around the pain, and now she's a treasure to me. She's part of who I am."

Like a pearl.

He thought of Krynn. If he let losing her destroy him, he would be wasting the life she lived, the love she had given him.

"It's hard to let go," he pleaded.

"It's not letting go. It's holding close," Peter answered. "It's holding close and loving and treasuring and remembering, and letting the beauty overcome the pain."

Joran smirked through his trembling smile. His voice was husky, but he joked, "You're in the wrong career. Being a guard really doesn't suit you nearly as well as a poet."

Peter gave a low laugh.

Their hammocks swung gently as they lay there quietly together, waiting for the waves of sleep to wash over them.

CHAPTER SIXTEEN

The cooler season had begun, but since Captain Markus had changed their course southward, the nice weather held as they neared the tropical lands.

Joran did what was expected of him, and he didn't find it as hard to stay through his shift, or so difficult to be around Peter now. Sometimes he and the other sailors sparred or fenced, and he enjoyed the tightness of his muscles, the way all his senses went on high alert when he faced off with them.

"You're making a name for yourself with that sword," Tips told him once. "You might even gain a sailor nickname for your skill."

Joran smiled, feeling satisfied. He wouldn't mind having a sailor nickname, maybe. "As long as it's not 'Pillows'," he tossed back, grinning at the lumpy man who was named for his extra stomach mass.

Pillows snorted, "More like 'Serpent' with that quick devilish tongue, boy," he returned good-naturedly.

***

Captain Markus approached them. "We're making a stop in Bristia, men," he informed them. "We'll dock at Solwin in two days' time. Everyone gets leave this time – in shifts, of course."

Joran's lips pulled into a grin. That was meant for him, he knew.

"I'm not sure how long we'll be there, but I'll be following up on some leads about the Left-Handed."

Joran's good mood was overshadowed by the thought of the assassin. He glanced at Peter, who was watching him closely. He hadn't shared his suspicions with anyone, but he was determined to do his part to track him down. And then kill him.

***

Bristia was beautiful. Colors swam along the coast like sunspots on the ocean. Flowers, fruits, and birds peeked from the branches of the thick foliage. The water turned from indigo to cerulean to turquoise as they drifted toward shore.

The men drew cards to determine who would take the first day's leave. Joran wasn't with that group, which meant Peter wasn't either, but just being close to the warm, lush land had him in a good mood. Even laundry duty wasn't as bad as usual, with the next day's adventure and freedom to look forward to.

Joran stirred the men's clothes around with a thick wooden pole. "It's funny, I used to think the crew's quarters smelled bad."

"It does," Peter argued.

"But we can be thankful Captain enforces laundry day and bathing. Can you imagine if he didn't care about cleanliness?"

"Please don't make me imagine that," Peter wrinkled his nose, grinning.

"Have you ever been to Bristia?"

"Of course not. Even Terind was new to me."

"Do you think they eat as much fish here as these Terindian sailors do?"

Peter shrugged. "I think all sailors eat fish, but judging by Solwin's proximity to the ocean, yes, I would suppose they do."

Joran groaned. "I'd be happy if I never had to eat fish stew again, and I've only been here three months."

"I'd be happy if you helped scrub the clothes and stopped drooling toward the shore," Peter grumbled.

***

The next morning Joran was up early, though he still didn't beat Peter out of bed. He pulled on fresh clothes, hung his sword sheath around his waist, and practically ran for the gangplank.

Captain Markus called out to him before he got very far. "Hold up, Joran. I have something for you." He waved a letter.

Joran turned back, his brows drawing together. Who would write to him?

"I picked it up at the port yesterday. I've tried to keep King Henry abreast of our route, especially with the changes."

Joran frowned down at the letter. It simply said his name on the front. He turned it over. His father's seal stared back at him. His heart sank, and the sunny morning no longer seemed so bright.

He nodded tightly at the Captain and stuck the letter in his waistband, trying to make himself pretend it wasn't there.

"Also, you may want your quarterly wages before you head out," the Captain suggested to him and Peter, who had caught up.

Captain Markus handed them each a coin pouch and Joran's brows shot up.

"I get wages?"

The Captain's rough white beard twitched as he smiled. "You're part of my crew now and you work for a wage, just like anyone else."

"Oh." He peered down eagerly at the coins. Money of his own. Money he had earned. He closed his fist around the metal pieces and grinned.

"Thank you, sir," Peter remembered, and Joran looked up guiltily and nodded his thanks along. A thrill raced through him. This day was going to be fun.

He wasn't prepared to stagger when he took his first few steps on land. Spirits, the ground seemed to be floating. Even Peter, as stiff as ever, stumbled a bit, but the sights and smells around them soon distracted Joran. A market sprawled out from the dock, which was crowded with sailors and merchants and peddlers. Most of the people were dark-skinned, and although they spoke the language of Kerrynth, they had a strong lilting accent which made it difficult to understand in passing.

"Maniv must be from Bristia," he commented to Peter.

He strolled through the market, keeping an eye out for something he wanted to spend his wages on. There were fabrics with dizzying patterns and blinding colors laid out on tables. The pungent smell of salted fish wafted from the next row of vendors, mixed with strong, unknown spices that were being dished out of cloth bags at a table ahead.

"Are you hungry?" He asked Peter. Better smells than fish beckoned him forward. He stopped at a table layered with triangular pastries. A young woman swished a cloth methodically in the air, keeping the flies off her treats. A headcovering, the color of fire, was draped over her hair. Joran had never seen such a brightly-colored fabric before. It complemented her deep skin tone and dark eyes. Dark eyes, which she blinked at him slowly. A golden ring hung from her nose, and Joran stared at the oddity.

"These look good," Peter said, jarring his thoughts. Joran smiled at the girl and paid for two pastries.

He peered curiously at the filling after his first bite. The pastry itself was light and mildly sweet, but the filling was what mesmerized him. "What is this?"

Peter chewed slowly. "Some kind of fruit, but I couldn't tell you what. It's tart."

"It's heavenly. The bakers at the castle need to learn how to make these."

Bristia was unlike anywhere he'd ever been.

A booth caught his eye. Jewelry hung from hooks all along the walls, mostly shells and glass, but there in the corner – pearls. Joran slowed, his eyes running over the muted beads. They seemed to glow with subtle colors – gray, pink, yellow.

The seller smiled widely at him, showing two missing teeth. The man had a black mustache and a red scarf tied around his head. "The pearls catch your eye. For a young maiden, perhaps? A miracle of the seas!" He waved his hand toward the collection proudly. "Have you seen my greatest treasure? A black pearl. Just brought in yesterday, all the way from the Smyer Isles."

He pulled a small box from under the table and opened it dramatically. There was a pearl there, a small one, but the hue was much darker than the others. It was a deep gray, with purple iridescence glimmering in the sunlight. The Smyer Isles were known for their pearl exports, and they traded freely with Kerrynth, so Joran relaxed. These weren't smuggled jewels. He glanced at the slightly tilted booth and cheaper jewelry and realized that this seller wasn't in the position to buy those kinds of goods anyway.

Joran wished Peter wasn't shadowing him right now. He wanted the pearl, but he didn't have a good reason to explain why.

I'm the bloody prince, he reminded himself.

"How much?" he demanded.

The man showed his missing teeth again and named a price. Joran frowned at him and stated a lower price. The man's face fell in an exaggerated pout.

"It's small," Joran pointed out.

"Ah, ok, for you my friend. I will give you a special discount."

They settled at a price just slightly higher than Joran had been hoping for, but he was satisfied.

"Here, so it doesn't get lost," the man said, handing him a thin leather strip, with a tiny cage of leather pieces at the bottom. He slid the pearl into the net, demonstrating, then pulled the two ends of the strap, tightening the net around the jewel at the bottom.

Joran thanked him, attaching the leather strings to his sheath belt.

He felt the questions in Peter's gaze as they continued on, but thankfully, he didn't press.

***

Joran gave the waitress his most charming smile as he held up his empty tumbler. She was at least fifteen years older than him, and rather portly, not that he minded that. She blushed and hurried over to refill his cup.

The Swordfish was a large tavern. It was a much nicer place than most Joran had visited. Tables and chairs weren't in pieces, there were enough lamps to light the whole place, and the floor wasn't filthy. It was popular too. Almost every table was full. Peter sat with him, sipping at water while Joran downed his ale. It burned his throat deliciously, and he had no plans to stop until he was stumbling drunk. They would be here a while.

He hadn't forgotten about the letter tucked into his pants, although he had been pushing thoughts of it aside all day.

He didn't want to hear from King Henry. His father had never listened to him, for as long as he could remember. He could blame the spell if he wanted, but if Joran had figured out his mother's magic just a few months after she first used it on him, the King should have been able to figure it out after years of ruling by her side. King Henry hadn't even heard him when he was pleading with him for Krynn, and when she died, well, he wasn't sure the man had even realized what had happened. He hadn't protected his sons from his wife's evil magic. Then, when he came to his senses, he finally looked at Joran and all he had seen was an embarrassing, disgusting boy. His cheek tingled with the phantom slap in his memory. His father had sent him away because he couldn't stand the sight of him. He wasn't about to allow that to happen again by opening the letter like he cared what his father thought. He wasn't ready to be lectured or checked up on to see if he was behaving. And he certainly wasn't about to admit that his father's plan to cast him out to sea to help him grow up, might actually be working.

He rubbed his forehead and fingered the edge of the letter with his other hand. The drinks weren't working fast enough. He needed another distraction.

Peter had a glass of water. Joran smirked at him. "Too young for the real stuff?" he goaded.

Peter didn't reply.

Joran clenched his jaw as the familiar irritation raised the hairs on his neck.

He pushed his mug in front of Peter. "Drink, you spirits-blasted puppy," he growled.

"I don't drink," Peter said mildly, edging the mug back toward the prince.

"You're scared."

"I made a vow."

Joran hooted. "A vow? Not to drink? What is wrong with you?"

Peter just raised his eyebrows. "My stepfather. He hurt us when he was drunk. I hated strong drinks and I vowed I would never lose my mind to them like that."

Joran huffed, gulping his own drink for good measure. He let the warm cloud fill his mind a bit and motioned the waitress over. She was too pleased. Her bright, painted lips repulsed him, but he took her hand and pulled her down to sit with him. He was determined to do something to fight down the rising anger and bitterness that his father's letter had sparked. He stroked the woman's cheek with a lazy fingertip.

Peter looked uncomfortable. "You've had enough, haven't you?" he asked.

Joran muttered a curse in his direction. He'd have to get rid of this breathing conscience. He winked at the woman. "Come back in a little bit, darling," he drawled, the slur partly genuine.

She giggled and pranced away.

Joran's eyes roamed the place, and he smiled when he found something even better than he had hoped. At a table, on the other side of the room, a pretty young lady sat by herself. He took in the mostly-male crowd in the tavern. That wouldn't last long. He wanted to go to her himself, but Peter would just follow.

He turned to his guard. "Have you ever kissed a girl?"

Peter actually blushed.

He appraised Peter. Tall, lithe, a long, fine nose, and dark brows. His eyes were as black as the sea at night. "Come on, a gentleman like you means to tell me he's never kissed a woman?"

Peter cleared his throat. "I think to get that far, you have to talk to her first, and I haven't had a lot of practice with that."

Joran pointed with his eyes in the direction of the girl sitting alone. "Tonight is the night that is going to change all that," he said, an eyebrow raised in a smirk.

Peter flicked a quick glance over his shoulder.

"Go. Now. Go talk to her. I'll bet you can't kiss her before the night's over," he challenged.

Peter rolled his eyes.

"I mean it. It's not often a young woman sits by herself in a tavern, and I guarantee it won't be that way much longer, so this is your spirits-given opportunity." He shoved Peter's arm.

Peter sighed. "I'll go if you promise to stop after this drink," he pointed at the half-empty tumbler on the table.

Joran groaned. "It's not your job to be my conscience," he complained.

Peter shrugged and waited.

"Fine, fine. I won't have any more. Just go." He waved Peter off.

Peter stood, straightened his shirt, and brushed nervous hands down his pant legs. His nose scrunched as he smoothed the hair down his neck. It had grown in the past few months, unruly over his ears and collar now.

Finally he turned and headed to the lonely table across the room, each step painfully stiff. Joran smirked to himself. Peter was so awkward it was adorable. He watched with amused interest as Peter approached the girl.

The chubby waitress sidled up to the table again, and Joran fought the urge to sigh in frustration. He forced a wide smile, and pulled her close as he gulped the last of his drink.

"Would you do me a favor, darling?" he mumbled close to her ear.

She blinked and reddened and nodded.

He pulled the letter from his waist and slid it toward her. "Throw this away for me?"

He stood, caressing her cheek with his thumb and winking. He usually wasn't above this kind of flirtation, but playing with her like this was turning his stomach. *Spirits. What is wrong with me?*

He walked away from the table, not turning back to see if the woman was disappointed or what happened to the letter.

There was a game going on, and he intended to join. Surely the tension and focus of cards would distract him. He glanced toward Peter, who was actually sitting at the table. The girl was smiling. Well. Maybe he had it in him after all.

A whimper caught his attention. He swung toward the sound. A young boy was clenching his jaw hard, though his eyes looked shiny with tears. A huge man stood beside him, his fearsome hand wrapped around the boy's arm. Hard.

"Shut up. You'll eat after you get the package for me. You work for me now, and no work – no food." He spit the words from the side of his mouth. If Joran had been any further away, he wouldn't have heard them.

He didn't know what was going on, but it couldn't be a good situation. The boy looked scared. The man was obviously hurting him.

Joran didn't think. He swung before he even realized what he was doing.

CHAPTER SEVENTEEN

The punch threw the man's head back, loosening his grip on the child, but barely rocking his heavy stance.

"Run," Joran commanded the boy while the man growled. He ducked to miss the man's reactive throw.

The place erupted.

More men leaped to their feet, surrounding Joran. He backed away and stumbled into a chair. He grabbed it, holding it like a shield in front of himself as he continued back tracking.

Someone from the side twisted the chair from his grip, slamming it down on the ground so hard a leg cracked.

There was shouting. People crowded each other to hurry away.

Something hit Joran in the jaw and he lost his vision for a moment. Another punch landed in his stomach and he doubled over, gagging.

He shoved his heel back, connecting with someone. From the howl that went up, it had been a good hit. He gasped for breath, trying to see past the colors in his vision. Where was the boy? Had he run?

Then Peter's face came into focus.

"Joran, let's go," he demanded from the edge of the circle.

The giant man glowered toward the new voice, his interest finding a new object.

Joran tried to choke out a warning, but he only managed a strangled sound before the man had shoved Peter so hard he hit the floor.

Joran lunged toward the man who was already poised to pummel Peter. He jumped on his back, tightening an arm around his thick neck.

"First punch was for the boy. This is for my friend," Joran snarled in his ear.

The massive man gurgled and tugged at Joran's arms, backing up to slam Joran against the wall. He heard the crack as his head hit. Pain shot through him.

Someone else peeled him off the man's back and landed a fist in his eye. He returned the blow, but his mind wasn't on the fight.

He had to help Peter.

Suddenly he landed on his back on the filthy floor. He scrambled up, gasping for air, and tore his sword loose from its sheath.

There was a shout as guards swarmed the tavern. Uniformed guards. City guards.

Joran's arms were quickly pinned from behind, and so were most of the other men's. He glanced through the door the guards had entered and saw the boy's face peering around the corner. He met Joran's gaze and held it for a second before turning and disappearing into the dark.

He'd called the city guards.

Joran hoped he would be able to get far away from the band who had brought him here.

***

The Captain's face was as fierce as Joran had ever seen it as he regarded Joran and Peter. Peter's lip was split, the blood already clotting in a messy lump. Joran could feel his eye swelling shut, and he ached everywhere.

"Your first night off in three months and you get thrown out of a tavern! No, dragged out – by the city guard no less! Even my wildest men know better than to get in a drunken brawl for no good reason."

Joran tightened his sore jaw, and tried not to stumble with the sway of the ship. The ale had finally soaked in.

The Captain didn't miss it. "You were obviously drinking like —"

"What, like a sailor?" Joran laughed coarsely.

"You, Prince Joran, after all your father has done to help you better yourself, are still determined to wallow in the pits the first chance you get. I thought I had seen some improvement in you, but I was wrong." Captain Markus' voice shook with restrained anger.

"And Peter, where were you when this began? Isn't it your job to keep the Prince out of trouble? Were you also drunk?" His glaring, blue eyes fell on Peter.

"I was distracted, sir. I am sorry," he said simply, lowering his head respectfully.

Joran grimaced. It was his fault Peter was distracted. He had pushed him away, and Peter had only gone so he would stop drinking, but, of course the young guard wouldn't stand up for himself.

I was just trying to help a kid, Joran wanted to shout, but he knew it wouldn't do any good.

"You are part of the Pearl's crew," the Captain reminded them. "You represent me and my honor on the seas. We are not a rogue pirate ship, boys. We work for the Terindian Guard. I will have to decide what to do with you."

He turned smartly on his heel, striding away.

"Sir?"

Joran jerked his head toward Peter.

"I understand that we handled ourselves shamefully, especially me for getting distracted from my duty. But, although Joran did initiate the first blow, he was defending a child who was being mistreated by a man in the tavern." He looked down. "With all respect, sir, I thought you should know that."

Captain Markus drew himself up, but uncertainty flickered in his eyes. "Get to bed. We'll discuss this tomorrow." He gave a curt nod and disappeared.

***

It was painful to get out of bed the next morning. Joran groaned as he hoisted himself out of the hammock. He wasn't sure how he'd be able to move, but he couldn't risk skipping his duties and incurring more of the Captain's wrath. As it was, he was nervous about the punishment he may have cooked up for them.

Peter was pulling on his boots.

"Not such an early riser after a night in a tavern?" Joran drawled.

"Still earlier than you," Peter shrugged.

Joran scowled and pinched his forehead. Spirits, his head hurt.

Peter was kneeling when Joran had finished dressing, and he waited awkwardly until his guard finished. He wanted to say something to him before they faced the Captain. Still, he couldn't resist a little teasing.

"I can't believe the only thing that could distract you from shadowing me is a pretty girl. I was beginning to think you were invincible."

"Hardly." Peter spoke mildly, tidying his quarters.

"It's just a pity I didn't give you a chance to kiss her before I started a fight." Joran winked.

Peter didn't respond.

"Unless, you already —"

"No."

"But you wanted to, didn't you? Tell me what she was like." He wiggled his eyebrows teasingly.

"You sound a little jealous," Peter smiled. "Maybe you should have been the one to meet her. Come on,

I'm sure the Captain will want to speak to us before work."

Joran sobered. "Peter, do you ever...regret becoming my guard?" he asked.

Peter stilled. He drew his brows together thoughtfully and tilted his head. "I don't regret it, Joran. I only regret failing you."

"Your record is good so far," Joran gave him his widest, dimpled smile, trying to lighten the moment. "Except for last night, but that was mostly my fault. As long as no more girls cross your path, you should be an excellent guard. If they do, just send 'em my way." He winked, wincing immediately afterwards.

Peter snorted. "You don't look as charming as you think, with your black eye. You'd better hope no girls cross your path right now."

They ascended the stairs together.

"Hey," Joran said. "Thank you for what you said to the Captain last night."

A small smile pulled at one side of Peter's face. "I just told him the truth."

CHAPTER EIGHTEEN

The day was long, every action a struggle, as Joran's bruises settled in. His headache raged for hours too. Still, he felt relieved. The Captain had been calmer that morning. Kind, even.

"With the information Peter volunteered, I've decided not to punish you too harshly. You did a good thing, Joran, standing up for the weak, even if you did it in the wrong way. You'll stay aboard ship for the rest of the time we're docked here, but after that, I see no reason to mention the incident again. Just take this as a warning and remember it for next time."

As it stood, they were casting off in two day's time anyway.

The men good-naturedly ribbed Joran about losing his mind in the drink, and he laughed along with them, teasing right back.

"It was Peter's fault," he said loudly as they gathered in the evening, making sure Peter heard him from his seat on the bottom stair. "You see, there was this maiden in the tavern all by herself, just swishing her hair and batting her lashes and practically begging for someone to put an arm around her. The spell she cast over Peter makes me think she was a siren."

"Sirens only live in the sea," Tips protested.

"Naturally, which is why she was such a sight, and why she felt so out of place. Well, Peter took one look, and he was smitten. He wobbled toward her like he was bewitched. He forgot all about me, and you know it's his duty to keep me straight," he winked here. The men guffawed, aware of Peter's tight adherence to rules.

"Of course, without my conscience, I was completely lost, stumbling around like a blind man. I fell headfirst into trouble, and the whole while Peter was in the corner, lost in her spell, staring at her like those fish stare back at me before I gut them."

More laughter. Even Peter shook his head and grinned.

"Is that her you're drawing, Peter?" Johnny asked, still teasing, as he stretched to see Peter's sketch. Peter smiled and regarded his paper before holding it up. "It's not. This is my grandfather. Got a letter from him in port, so he's been on my mind."

Peter's eyes met Joran's briefly, full of emotions Joran couldn't read, before he bent back over his work. The sailors nodded or grunted in appreciation. Joran's quick glance at the sketch was casual, but he was more impressed than he wanted to let on. Peter's grandfather looked kind, the firm lines of his face softened by thin wrinkles. His eyes were full of love.

The conversation drifted, but Joran snuck another curious glance toward Peter and his drawing. He could tell Peter's grandfather meant everything to him. Why hadn't he said anything about receiving a letter from him? Joran hadn't shared his own letter from King Henry just because he hadn't been happy to receive it, but it would have been different if it had been from someone who loved him. He shrugged to himself. Peter was just private that way. He watched as Peter finished and blew the lead dust from the paper before folding it carefully. He was glad Peter had his grandfather. He didn't seem to have much else. He deserved at least one good person in his life.

***

Joran was enjoying teasing Peter about the girl in the tavern, even if he could barely get a reaction out of him.

"This is getting old," Peter groaned the second night. They were already in bed. "There's nothing to tell. Her name was Catren. She was there with her cousin, who had joined the card game. We talked for about a whole minute before you had the place in uproar and the city guards after us."

"And?"

"And what? If you want to talk about girls, you do the talking. Tell me about someone you met."

Joran was silent. He'd flirted with plenty of girls since Krynn died, even been intimate with a fair number of them, but the only one who had ever mattered was Krynn. The ones who came after were merely a distraction from missing her.

He rubbed her ring on his pinky.

"It's not the same. I can't." he said quietly.

"Then talk about her."

He sighed. "I don't know...how do I talk about her? She was kind. She got embarrassed when I kissed her or called her beautiful, and it was adorable. She loved everyone, everything. One day she caught a beetle in her room and let it go outside so it wouldn't be killed. What girl does that? She especially loved birds, so I called her Birdie. Kind of why the tattoo..." He trailed off.

Peter sat up. There was still a lantern swinging near the stairs. Not everyone had bedded down yet.

"She sounds lovely," Peter said quietly.

"She was." Joran smiled, his eyes far away, reliving memories.

"I'm glad you had her, Joran. And I'm glad she had you."

Joran turned to look at his friend. "How can you say that? She'd hate me if she knew what I did." He let out a bitter laugh.

"You wouldn't have been like that if she had lived. You were just trying to deal with the pain of losing her."

Joran swallowed. Peter understood too much.

"That's not who you are, Joran. It's just how you coped. You loved her. You risked your life and position to admit you were in love with her. No one could ask for more than that. And you still take risks for good. You literally tried to fight a whole band of men to help one little boy just two nights ago. She was lucky to have your heart while she lived. The fact that it has been a year and you still love her only shows how devoted you were."

Joran tried to smile, but it was shaky.

He pressed his palms against his eyes until it hurt. Then he glanced at his guard.

"Thanks, Peter."

Someone finally extinguished the light, and Joran slid down into his hammock, glad for the darkness hiding his emotions.

***

A week back at sea passed. At dinner, the Captain addressed them.

"We're sailing out to the Smyer Isles, men. I got word in Bristia that the Left-Handed and his rogues use the smaller islands as a hideout."

Guilt tugged at Joran. He'd been so busy enjoying Bristia before getting himself in trouble and ruining his chances of enjoying it again, that he'd completely forgotten to cast about for information. He tried to focus on what the Captain was saying.

"There is a storm building ahead, and I'm changing course to see if we can backtrack and sail around it, but depending on how big it is, we may not have time. After dinner we prepare."

The other sailors seemed to know what to do, and they got busy as soon as they pushed away from the table.

Joran stood back, lost in the clamor of movement until someone handed him a bucket. "Swab the deck or we'll flood," Serb told him. Obediently, he began sloshing the water over the wooden planks, soaking them so they would swell and prevent leaking when the rain came. Men climbed the rigging and got into position, prepared to stow the sails once the Captain gave the signal. The Pearl was slowly changing direction, trying to circle around the storm. Others tied rope lengths to steady points along the deck, creating loops in the ends to hold the men to the ship if the weather got too bad. The crew scurried about, tying down supplies, moving things below decks, and reinforcing doors.

***

The storm was larger than the Captain had estimated, and a few hours later, they found themselves in the thick of it.

The wind howled, throwing the ship around with fury. Waves rose and fell, towering above the ship before plunging them down again. The Captain, tied securely, tried to keep his footing at the wheel. He fought to keep the ship on an angular course, tacking as the wind changed direction. Heading straight into the wind would likely shred their sails.

The rain hit before they were ready, slashing across the deck like daggers. The men in the ropes, trying to stow the sails, held on for dear life, barely able to lower the canvas.

"Give them anchor ropes!" The Captain shouted, his voice whipped away before he finished.

The experienced sailors already knew what to do without the command. They secured themselves first, lengthening the give, and began to ascend the rigging, trailing long rope anchors with them.

Someone shoved rope at Joran. "Secure yerself, boy," the man bellowed.

Joran gripped a pole, trying to plant his feet firmly enough to let go and pull the rope tight around his waist. The deck was slick, and the ship pitched mercilessly, making it hard to stand upright for even a second without holding on.

The sun was setting, darkness already hovering around them because of the clouds blocking out the last light.

The mainmast creaked loudly, and Joran jerked his head up. If that thing split, it could fall right on him. His feet slid, and the rope he had managed to wrap around himself caught, bringing him up short. Spirits, that bruised. He burned his hands grappling for a hold on the slick rope and dragging himself back upright.

The back sails had closed, lessening the pressure on the ship from the wind that had been caught in them. Just the two lower sails and the mainsail to go. The men above were fighting to hurry before the wind ripped right through the old canvas.

"Joran!"

Peter's voice came sharply through the wind. His face was frozen on something above Joran. Joran twisted, just in time to see a wooden beam flying toward him.

He jolted to the side, the pole careening past him. His eyes darted around. Where had that come from? Sailors shouted, though he couldn't make out what anyone was saying. The wind had caught the boom, loose now that the sails had been untied, and whipped it away from the men trying to secure it.

He stepped out of reach of the dangerous pole and turned to find Peter. He owed him a thank you.

Peter had drifted further. Sheets of rain shrouded the space between them. Peter was struggling to – spirits! He was holding onto his own rope anchor, but it wasn't fastened around him.

Joran lunged toward him. The bow of the ship plummeted, throwing him forward. His knees slammed into the deck, but he didn't feel the pain. He was frozen in horror. Peter was knocked off balance too, and he fell onto his stomach, sliding backward. He hung on to the swinging rope, terror splayed across his face. And then he was gone.

The rope was ripped from his hands, and it careened crazily across the deck, empty. Peter's body went flying toward the rail, which was no longer a barrier at this angle, with the ship pointed straight down.

Joran screamed.

He struggled to tear his rope off. It wasn't long enough. Peter couldn't swim.

Peter couldn't swim!

"Man overboard!" he shrieked. He slipped and slid toward the spot Peter had catapulted off the ship. Kirk grabbed him and he writhed, trying to free himself from the man's grip.

"Tie yourself," Kirk shouted into his ear. He produced a rope, a long one, and helped Joran tighten the knot around his waist. Every second was agony. Peter couldn't swim. Peter was in the water, the dark, angry water, drowning like his sister.

"I'll count to one hundred and pull you up," Kirk instructed.

Joran didn't hesitate a second more. He didn't have time for a plan. He hurled himself into the thrashing monster below.

He was a good swimmer. He had spent all his free time at the lake at home, and he could swim before he was five, but nothing prepared him for this. The middle of the ocean during a storm was nothing like a still lake.

The water was heavy, thick, and powerful. It hit him so hard it knocked the air out of his lungs. He gasped, fighting to gather breath so he could plunge down. A wave spilled over him, forcing water up his nose and shoving him under. He pushed deeper. The sea fought him like a devil, rolling and tossing him. The rope wrapped around his legs, and he kicked to free himself. He'd lost all sense of direction.

He couldn't see in the dark. He struggled forward. Out. Anywhere, stretching and feeling for his friend.

The rope began to pull, working with the waves to suffocate him. He couldn't stop now, but Kirk was pulling him up.

One hundred. He'd been disoriented for too long. Peter would die. His own lungs stung with need.

Air. Air. Air. He surged up with the tug of the rope, spluttering and sucking in air.

He could hear a voice from the distance, but he ignored it, letting the sea swallow him again before he'd even caught his breath.

He fought harder, though his arms and legs felt powerless against the current. Water surged around him, knocking into him, confusing him. It felt solid, tricking him into thinking he'd found Peter, only to dissipate in his clutch.

The One. Peter. Help. He prays.

The thoughts were disjointed, swirling across his consciousness like the sea.

Something brushed against him, something solid. He grabbed, and, unlike the water that left his fists empty, he was grasping cloth.

A body. He wrapped both arms around the figure, who was slanted oddly. Up, where was up? He tried to follow the rope, but the long length was twisted around him by the water, making the direction hard to follow.

He needed to breathe again. He'd let out too much air when the body had hit him. His eyes stung, and he squeezed them, blowing out the rest of his air and willing his body to rise.

The person in his arms was a dead weight dragging him down. He hugged tighter, but he didn't have the strength to hold on and swim.

Then he was gliding through the water, the rope being reeled in from above.

His head broke the surface, and he gulped in a breath, his arms still locked around the body. Around Peter.

Kirk and another man hefted them up. The rope crushed his middle, and holding on to Peter was the hardest thing he had ever done. Tears and sweat squeezed out, soaking him along with the rain. He would never let go, even if his arms fell off, but he screamed with the effort.

Then he hit the deck. Solid wood beneath him.

Peter lay beside him, face down on the floor, unmoving. Joran wanted to sit up. He wanted to shake his friend. But he couldn't move. Nothing worked.

Kirk bent over Peter, blocking Joran's view. He pulsed up and down, once, twice. Then he paused and drew back. He shot a strange look toward Joran, which he couldn't decipher, before resuming his effort to make Peter breathe.

It took a few minutes for Joran to catch his breath and get his arms and legs to work again. He felt as heavy as the mast. He dragged himself to a sitting position, trying to brace himself against the movement of the ship so he wouldn't slip away. The life-saving rope was still attached to him.

He crawled over to where Kirk was working. Peter coughed violently, his face screwed up tight, and Joran felt dizzy from relief.

Then he noticed.

Peter's shirt was torn open, all the buttons ravaged by the waves, and it hung off one shoulder, the sleeve gaping where the water had clawed at him.

At her.

Peter was a girl.

Dizziness hit Joran so hard, his legs gave out again, and he collapsed. He hit the deck hard and didn't know anything else.

CHAPTER NINETEEN

When Joran finally awoke, it was still dark, but the storm had softened. He could hear rain, but it wasn't hitting him. The sides of his hammock rose above him. He was below decks.

Still, the storm didn't seem as fierce. He hadn't been flung out of his bed.

Everything came rushing back. Black seawater, the roaring in his ears, his death grip on Peter.

Peter. A girl.

Bile rose in his throat.

He was in so much pain.

He closed his eyes, too sore to move, too tired to think. Blessed sleep claimed him again.

***

Serb visited him later in the morning. Joran was awake, and the ship rocked with usual calm, so he knew they had made it through the storm. But his core was so bruised and his arms so sore he couldn't force himself to sit up.

"Looking bad, mate," Serb greeted him, rubbing his scruffy black beard.

"Thanks," he croaked.

"We live, as you can tell," he updated him. "Storm didn't pass until about four this morning, but the Captain pulled us through. The mainsail was damaged, but it's repairable."

He rubbed his beard again nervously.

Joran didn't want to hear what he was going to say. "I need water," he managed instead.

Serb nodded and left, returning with a cup a minute later.

Joran swallowed ravenously, the water cooling his parched throat.

"Your guard. He, ah, he's in Kirk's cabin. Captain thought it best for now. He means to speak with you both soon."

Joran let his eyes fall shut. So Peter was alive. He was relieved. And scared.

He couldn't forget what he had seen. Kirk knew too. He remembered the strange look he had sent him.

"I'll let the Captain speak with you then, when he's recovered a bit too," Serb said, retreating hastily.

Joran watched him go. Serb knew too, he could tell.

He wanted to know the story, wanted to know why just as much as he didn't. He'd risked his life to save Peter, only to find out that he hadn't saved Peter at all. He didn't even know Peter.

He cursed.

***

He wasn't feeling much better the following morning. If anything, he felt even stiffer, but the Captain himself descended the stairs, and Joran grit his teeth to sit up.

Captain Markus held up his hand. "Prince Joran, you're exempt from your duties today. I imagine you're still finding it hard to move."

Joran nodded.

"You were courageous and selfless the other night. If it weren't for you, your guard wouldn't have lived. No one else saw the fall." His face relaxed into something like a smile.

Joran just nodded again.

"However, there are some things that we must discuss immediately. Please change and meet me upstairs in the first mate's cabin."

"It's about Peter," Joran said, his voice still scratchy.

The Captain's eyebrow lifted. Joran stood, even the soles of his feet hurting when he planted them on the floor.

"It is."

"Peter is a woman," he bit out. He didn't need people to beat around the bush, act like he didn't know. He just wanted to get the truth out.

Still, the words in the air hit him like a slap.

"Yes. Get dressed. We'll discuss it together."

Joran dressed. Fresh clothes felt heavenly after the damp ones he'd had on since the storm, not that it made it any easier to get into them.

Woodenly, he climbed the stairs, ignoring the stares from the other men on deck. Spirits. Everyone knew, and they were all looking at him like he'd had something to do with it - like maybe he'd known all along and had been bunking next to a woman on purpose.

Anger washed over him.

Of Oceans and Pearls

The Captain met him, and they entered the first mate's cabin, the place Joran had spent his first miserable week at sea. The sight of the bunk brought back dark memories, and he shook his head before the feelings of nausea and withdrawal came back too.

Peter lay there now, the rough blanket pulled over him – her – all the way to her chin. Her black eyes were open and alert, and she looked...scared.

A muscle in his jaw twitched.

The Captain sat on a stool, and motioned Joran over to the coils of rope in the corner, the place Peter had claimed when they were there before.

Joran sat.

Captain Markus spoke. "Peter, you can thank the One and Joran for saving your life. He was the only one who saw you fall, and he dived in after you, found you in that chaos, and hauled you back on board."

Peter's eyes flickered over to Joran's face and away.

The Captain cleared his throat.

"However, Peter, you were unconscious when you got back on board. Kirk worked to bring you back. During that time, he and a few others noticed that you aren't who you've led us to believe. Would you mind telling us what is going on? Perhaps you could start with your name," he added gently, when the fear in Peter's eyes flared.

Peter's face clouded.

"My name is Petra," she said. Joran was surprised that she still sounded like the Peter he knew. Her voice was low and even, the same voice that had spoken to him through the dark many times as they lay side by side in their hammocks.

The Captain nodded. "Petra." He looked at Joran. "Were you previously aware that Petra is a woman?"

Joran flushed. "Of course not." He glanced at Petra, his embarrassment flashing into anger.

"Petra, this is quite a serious lie. Pretending to be a man for the past three months is not only a moral issue, but it also put you in an inappropriate situation." He glanced at Joran. "Not to mention my men."

"I'm sorry, Captain," she said. "I can explain, and I know it was wrong for me to deceive you." Her black eyes filled with tears.

"Until now, you've been a model crew member, Petra. Please explain yourself," Captain Markus demanded, though not harshly.

Joran ground his teeth together.

He'd trusted Peter. He'd loved him. Peter was his first friend in years, and he'd told him everything, but Peter was Petra, and Petra had lied. Lied about the most fundamental part of herself and lied every single day for months.

"I am Cleftan," she began. His gaze jerked to her face, and he glared. He'd believed she was from Ethereal, hired as a royal guard by his father. Betrayal, that's what this was. Deception and outright betrayal.

"My grandfather, Captain General Rehara, is from Cleft. My mother ran away when she was a young woman to marry a man my grandfather didn't approve of. She crossed the border into Ethereal, and that's where I was born," she clarified. She darted another look at Joran. "I told you this part. My father left us before I was born. My mother didn't want to go home defeated, so she remarried, and my stepfather was a heavy drinker. He beat her and hurt me."

Pain flitted across her expression.

"I had a sister who died when she was six." Again she looked at Joran as if for confirmation, but he wouldn't give it. He couldn't. How could he believe anything she had said?

"Then my mother died when I was twelve. I ran away from home and tried to find my grandfather, the only relative I knew about. It took me a long time to get back to Cleft and locate him. I was thirteen when I found him. He took me in, and when I was sixteen, he allowed me to join the army."

"He asked you to hide your identity?" Captain Markus sounded his disapproval.

Petra shook her head quickly. "No, no he didn't. Women can be soldiers in Cleft, though it's not typically a position most women choose. I wanted to make my grandfather proud. I was happy to join under his command. He taught me well. He'd been teaching me defensive techniques for a few years already before I became a soldier."

She tucked her hair behind her ears nervously. Such a feminine motion. Had she always done that?

"Last year, my division was sent into Ethereal on a confidential mission. We met with the Great Magister in secret. He had summoned us because one soldier in our division was gifted. The Great Magister wanted to gain our trust and have us locate a magical crystal that was hidden in Cleft and bring it to him. Things went downhill from there. On our return to Cleft from Ethereal, two of the men in our group took control. They murdered the gifted soldier to eliminate his power and made the rest of us swear loyalty to them or be killed as well."

She pushed herself up farther on the bed.

"I took the oath in order to survive, but I didn't mean it."

Lies. Again. She can't be trusted.

"I was devoted to helping the remaining gifted in Ethereal gain freedom. The Great Magister and many of the gifted were banished long ago, and they'd been living in hiding ever since. There aren't many people with gifted abilities in Cleft, but those who do call the town their home are free to exist without fear. My baby sister, Lia, was gifted." Her dark eyes pierced Joran, snapping with something defensive. "Lia could fly. She was just learning about her gift. She was *my* birdie. One day she flew over the pond, but when she looked down and realized how far she had drifted, she got scared and fell. That's why I couldn't reach her."

The Captain cleared his throat, drawing her attention back to the narrative.

"The two men who had taken over our band deserted the army, and we, sworn to them for our lives, followed. Eventually they found the crystal in Cleft. The Great Magister had told us that the crystal we were after was part of a set of three that once united, held immeasurable power. Of course the miscreants wanted all of them. They attacked Haven to get the crystal there, though they never ended up getting their hands on it. Another crystal was in Ethereal. I worked as a spy for the Great Magister, pretending to be part of the rogue clan, and informed him of their plans as often as I could."

A memory surged in Joran's mind. During the revolt a few months ago, Magister Erlich had acquired all three green crystals. One had been Queen Lilian's, the source of her power. The second one was Princess Avalon's. Three soldiers from Cleft had arrived just after the revolt, bringing the crystal from their kingdom, the final one in the set. One soldier had long black hair. Joran had only seen a glimpse of them, but he'd thought it strange that a woman was a soldier.

He studied Petra's black hair, which had grown bushy and uneven since they'd left Terind a few months ago; when they had stepped first onto the Pearl it had been closely cropped to her head. But it had been long before that. He remembered seeing it sway past her hips that morning at Blackstone Castle.

"When the Magister suggested King Henry send Joran to serve at sea, the King wanted a guard, but the other guards were wary to do it – trust was an issue at that time with most of the royal guards. Magister Erlich told the King about me, and King Henry asked if I would do it. I'd deserted the Cleftan army, and no matter the reasons, I knew I'd not be welcomed back to my post." She sighed. "I was afraid to go back to my grandfather after what I'd done. True soldiers should die honorably, not defect to save their own lives, which is how I feared my grandfather would see my desertion. But I knew I couldn't agree to such a responsibility just to secure myself a post. It had to mean something to me. I asked the King to tell me everything about you, Prince Joran. When I saw how emotionally distraught he was about you, I wanted to help him. And the more he told me about you, the more I wanted to help you too. It became more than a job for me. So he commissioned me for the task."

She snuck another glance at Joran. "My grandfather wasn't quite the reason I got this job, but I still feel like I owe him for it since he trained me. Otherwise I wouldn't have been qualified..." her eyes fell as anger snapped in Joran's.

Petra took a deep breath and looked to the Captain.

"I knew the Prince would never respect me or accept me if I showed up as a girl, and I knew my chances of getting on board a ship as a woman were low, so I disguised myself. No one asked me to do it, but I felt it was the only way I could fulfill my duty."

"I never needed a *girl* protecting me," Joran spat.

"I'm sorry. It was wrong, but your father and the Great Magister wanted to know you were safe. I wanted you to be safe too, to have someone who cared, and I couldn't come up with another way." Her voice was pleading.

Joran shoved to his feet, his muscles crying out in protest. "Look, *Petra,*" he let ice coat the words. "I may have been a drunk, and a drug user, and a gambler, but at least I never lied about who I was."

The Captain opened his mouth. Petra looked stricken. But he wasn't finished, "Darn right I wouldn't want a girl protecting me. I didn't need anyone, and I still don't. Don't ever come near me again. Spirits, I should have let the sea take you to your sister when it tried."

He stomped to the door, flinging it open. He wanted to get away, but the Pearl suddenly felt small. He couldn't hide. There was nowhere to truly be alone.

He hated her.

Maybe he didn't mean that he wished she had died, but, by the spirits, he was so angry, that maybe he did.

CHAPTER TWENTY

Captain Markus decided to head up the coast and make a stop at Hollowsprit, the capital city of Terind, before pursuing the criminal pirate to the Smyer Isles. It was the closest port, and the ship needed some repairs as a result of the storm. The water that had seeped under doors and sloshed down the stairs had ruined a good bit of supplies that would need to be restocked too.

Maniv complained about the lack of flour, but fish stew was the same with or without bread. The men patched up the mainsail, and the Pearl skimmed the waters toward Hollowsprit.

Joran's own bag of belongings had gotten drenched the night of the storm. Although the door to the hatch had been secured shut, water had found a way underneath.

"Curse the spirits," he moaned. At the bottom of the bag, packed securely beneath his clothes, was the stack of Krynn's letters he had grabbed before he'd been hurried away from the castle. He hadn't read them for a long time. It always hurt too much, but having them close was comforting. Grief slammed into his chest as he pulled them out now. The papers were soft and heavy with moisture, beginning to tear apart where his fingers gripped them.

"No, no, no." The words had been obliterated, the ink just macabre smears across the pages.

His pearl was there too, still in the leather cage at the very bottom of his satchel. He picked it up, rubbing the smooth orb between his fingers, wishing the legends were true. Wishing he could believe in some easy trick that would make everything better. But it was just a jewel. He flung it back into his bag. It wasn't fair that it had remained unblemished, while the things that mattered most to him had been destroyed.

When evening came, Joran was first to the tables below decks. He filled a mug with ale and chugged it. He hadn't tried to drink on board since the first night, but spirits help him if anyone tried to stop him now.

The men filed in lazily, pouring their own drinks and leaning back. Conversation floated – the usual, and Joran droned it out. He didn't pay attention to anything until Kirk stopped him as he was pouring another drink.

"That's enough, mate."

Joran spat and shrugged off the hand on his arm.

The table quieted.

"Kirk, he's a storm stomper. You saw what he did that night. Give him a break," Pillows said.

Kirk eyed Pillows, but didn't answer him. "That's not what this is for," he said to Joran, taking his mug and setting it down out of reach.

Joran curled his lip at the first mate and cursed. "You all drink every night," he hissed. "I'm not a child. Give me a cup."

Kirk caught his arm mid-swing and forced it down on the table. He leaned in close, his rugged face narrowed and threatening. "If you want a drink to pass the time and lighten the mood, you're welcome in this group, but we don't drink away our problems. You've got to face your problems head-on, boy. Nothing in these barrels will solve them for you."

Joran's other fist clenched. Anger shook his shoulders.

Kirk laid an iron grip there too. "By the way, resorting to anger every time you feel something you don't want to feel isn't going to help either. Get to the bottom of your feelings, Joran, and deal with them. You think you're angry at the girl, but maybe you're not. Maybe it's something else."

He shoved Joran toward the stairs.

***

The crew seemed eager to talk to him about his rescue, but he ignored their questions. It wasn't something he wanted to think about. "You'll be a legend, boy," Tips offered in his crackly voice. "Those who enter the sea during a storm like that rarely survive. If they do, we call them a storm stomper."

Johnny grinned. "Looks like we found you a name, Stomper. And we thought it would come from your blade swinging."

"Kirk pulled me up," Joran said dully. Not even his sudden heroism could lighten his mood right now. He pushed away from the table. "So he's the reason I lived."

***

As soon as they docked, Joran left the ship. He didn't bother looking for Petra. He hadn't seen her for the past two days. Apparently she had taken over Kirk's cabin, as Kirk had moved into her vacant hammock beside Joran. He wasn't going to have her trying to follow him, that was for sure.

Kirk was right about one thing, though Joran would never admit it – not even to himself – he hated that Peter was a fake, hated that he'd opened up and trusted a girl. He hated that his life had been confounded, that his insides were full of complicated emotions. And he hated that he couldn't get the sight of Petra, half-dead, lying on the deck with her clothes hanging off, and her perfect, little breasts bared to the sky, out of his mind. He could still see the rain running off her pale skin, down the petite mounds, her perky nipples erect in the cold. Spirits, how he hated that memory. Because the image was insanely beautiful, and he wanted to see it again.

Kirk was right that there was something more than anger there, but the feeling was something he didn't want. Anger was much easier to trust.

He'd never been to Hollowsprit, but it almost looked like his home in Ethereal. Terind had the same beautiful forests as Ethereal. His mother was from Terind, and most of her family still lived in the protectorate kingdom. He rubbed his forehead as he walked, his head down. An hour's ride west of here would probably bring him to Glensprit, where Aunt Adeline and Lady Marty lived. He was only a few miles away from Krynn's body right now. He hadn't been so close to her since her body had been sent to her own mother for burial.

There was too much going on in his head and heart. He had his own storm beating him up from the inside out, and he had to do something to release some of the pressure. He wandered away from the busy, main streets, heading in the opposite direction of the wealthier homes. Soon the larger, two-story homes gave way to rows of ramshackle houses crowded together. Rancid smells rose from the piles of garbage between buildings. He was thankful for the plain sailor's clothes he wore. Although his shirts and breeches had been fine ones from home when he'd boarded ship, months of work and wear had made them as common as the other men's. His attire helped him blend in a lot better in a place like this than when he was dressed as a prince.

He whispered to a dodgy man, who whispered back. "After dark," he'd said. It was still several hours until then, but Joran had nothing else to do. He found an empty alley and sank down to the cobblestones to wait.

When the sun had finally set, Joran got up and stretched. He followed the man's directions to an empty house three streets over. A female form stepped in front of him, cooing up at him, but he shook his head and walked on. The place really did look abandoned from the outside. The wooden slats were split and weathered. A few hung loosely, and the roof thatching was molded. Chunks of the roof were missing in places. He glanced around before heading to the back entrance. A man searched him before letting him in, collecting Joran's entry fee.

The fights had already begun. Two men were circling each other. Joran joined the group of onlookers. Two dim lamps gave off just enough light to make out the figures pouncing on each other. Joran watched their moves closely. They were older than him, and not too skilled, although they had some power. Still, if he was matched with one of these men, it would be easy. The crack of a jaw resounded through the empty space, and the crowd gave a collective gasp. A man fell back, his head hitting the stone floor with a sickening thud. A deep calm settled over Joran. He took a deep breath and blinked languidly. This would be good. This would help. He'd welcome the pain of a split lip or the searing hot flash of a fist in his nose. Adrenalin started flowing, filling him with energy.

Joran was placed in the third match. His opponent was a wiry man, taller than he was, and a few years older. The fighter moved quickly. His speed was his power. Joran sidestepped a blow and continued sizing him up. He was like lightning on his feet, but he left his middle unprotected. A smile crossed Joran's lips and he gave a false swing, causing the lean man to jerk to the side and then he sent his boot crashing into his opponent's gut, catching him off guard.

The fight was over too soon. The tall man had gone down easily. Joran rolled and unrolled his fists as the call was announced, almost disappointed at having to stop. But the cheers from the crowd eked out a grin, and he let it spread until he could feel his dimple as he headed to the manager to collect his prize.

Street fighting was illegal in Ethereal, and it was obviously the same here, judging from how the contests were hidden here. It was probably due in part, to the various items people traded for entry fees or received in winnings. Still, he wasn't expecting the pouch the manager placed discreetly in his palm.

The man glanced around from under lowered brows. "It's a hefty value, but I pay well for skill. Young blood like you excites the crowd. I hope you'll perform for us again."

Joran nodded, unable to keep his eyes off the prize. He turned his back to the crowd as the audience focused on the next match, and pinched the pouch open. Gray powder was nestled inside. His heart raced.

Jacin.

Joran squeezed the pouch in his hand as he walked back toward the harbor. The soft shifting of the powder in the cloth was soothing. He didn't want it. He never wanted to be under its influence again or suffer the way he had while his body was adjusting to being without it. His own mother had helped bring this destruction into Kerrynth, and he wanted nothing to do with it. He hated jacin.

And he'd never wanted something so much in his life.

CHAPTER TWENTY-ONE

A Terindian festival was starting tomorrow, and the Captain said they would stay docked for the week of festivities. It would give them time to restock the ship and do the necessary repairs, and those who had family in Terind might visit them or at least write.

Joran wasn't familiar with the Terindian holiday, but the men were excited to be on land for it. Pillows seemed downright gleeful. "I got a girl here whose family is putting on a feast tomorrow night. She's invited the lot of us, since we're in town."

"You've got a girl?" someone yelled.

"She's the best one of the bunch, too," he bellowed back. "All right, all right, she's my cousin, but the invitation is real."

The men howled with laughter. Everyone bathed that afternoon and dressed in clean clothes. Pillows told them the family was well-off. Joran surveyed his beard in the warped reflection of the tin plate the men used as a mirror.

"Need a shave?" Tips offered.

He tilted his head. "It has grown on me," he quipped. "I think I'll keep it, but a trim might do the trick."

The sun was setting as the merry crew descended the gangplank. Joran threw a glance back to the Pearl, bobbing proudly in the shallow water, and stilled. Petra was standing on the ramp above them. She looked like Peter. Like she hadn't changed, and his stomach churned unpleasantly. She met his gaze, but waited until he'd turned away and continued with the others, before moving to follow them from a distance.

Pillows led them to a large house. It wasn't as impressive as most of the places Joran had frequented as royalty, but the family obviously lived in a social tier above the rest of the sailors. Pillow's cousin, Vara, was plain, but pleasant. She lived there with her parents. Pillows made the introductions awkwardly, but she smiled at them all.

"Welcome to Emberton Hall," she said warmly. "We're honored to celebrate Night of Fire with you brave men who protect our coasts."

Night of Fire was the first night of the Festival of Origins. Serb had explained it to Joran on the way there, though he'd only been half listening. The Festival was one of thanksgiving to the One for creating the Kingdoms of Kerrynth. Night of Fire, Night of Water, Night of Air... Joran couldn't remember the others.

The smell of roasted meat lingered in the air of the halls, tantalizing him. It had been too long since he'd had a real meal. He couldn't hide his pleasure as they ate. The pheasant was soft and savory on his tongue and he snuck another helping of roasted nuts because they were delectably sweet. After the meal, which was everything he had hoped for, tea was served, and then the chairs and tables were cleared to make room for dancing. "Until the bonfire is lit," the hosts promised. "Then we'll dance outside."

Joran lounged, too full to move. He'd wanted to make a point of avoiding Petra, but she had avoided him too, making his efforts futile. He hadn't seen her all evening. He shook the thoughts of her from his mind. Pillows was attempting to dance, his rolling form lumbering awkwardly as he tried to keep up. Joran fought a grin. At least the man was happy, judging from the smile splitting his heavy cheeks. Kirk, tall and gangly, made a surprisingly good dancer. He moved gracefully with Vara, his pock-marked face as serious as ever, but she looked genuinely pleased. Joran was caught up in watching the dancers, and he jumped when someone spoke into his ear.

"Joran, could we go somewhere? I need to talk to you." Peter's voice.

Petra.

He twisted to look up at her, his features darkening. Hers were a mask.

"I haven't seen you for a few days, but there are some things I'd like to tell you that I didn't want the Captain to hear." Her voice shook a little, or perhaps he was imagining it.

He considered refusing. Walking off. Ignoring her. *"You have to face your problems head-on, boy."* Kirk's voice sounded in his head.

He sighed and stood, gesturing with his palm. "Fine. Lead the way."

He followed her out of the large room and down an empty hall. No lights had been lit back here. They exited through a back door. It was strangely quiet. No one was around. The night air was frosty, and he shivered involuntarily as they stepped outside. Petra stopped a few feet ahead of him and turned around.

Her look was steady, but something unreadable flashed through her eyes.

"Petra, what —"

He didn't have a chance to finish. Something clamped over his lips. He twisted, realizing two shadowy figures had emerged from the bushes, pinning him. He searched desperately for Petra, but she had disappeared.

Something was shoved against his face, an acidic smell overwhelming his nostrils. Everything went blank.

***

Joran awoke on the floor of a horse-drawn cart. He struggled to sit up, but his hands and feet had been tied. A strip of cloth was tight across his mouth, cutting into his skin. He forced himself to breathe through his nose. *Breathe.*

The cart was speeding along and the bumps battered him. Two men sat guard on either side of him. They were armed. His eyes fell to their weapons. The man on his left eyed him threateningly.

"Where are you taking me?" Joran struggled to get the question out, but it was only a garbled sound behind the gag.

The toe of a boot hit his ribs. Hard. He flinched.

When the cart finally stopped, he tried to make out where they were, but it was too dark to see much. The men dragged him into a brick house, a standalone two-story mostly concealed by trees. There was no visible yard or path to the house, as though it had stood there for years without use.

They were met with complete darkness inside. The third man, who had been driving the cart, held a lantern ahead of them as they descended into the lower part of the house. The cold, stale air smelled like dirt. They were in a cellar.

The men shoved Joran, and he lost his balance, falling down hard on his tailbone. Pain soared through his back, and he grit his teeth.

The men wrenched his arms above his head as he stood, tying them to a hook in the beam above him. He couldn't move, couldn't even sit.

Curse the spirits.

The men left.

***

Joran stood in the prison of darkness, fighting down the terror that clawed up his throat. His arms ached already. The blackness was so thick, he couldn't see his elbow in front of his face. The wall of black seemed to grow contorted faces that twisted and leered at him. He screamed, though it was only a muffled breath. His cheeks were bruised from the tight cloth still tied around his mouth.

Hours passed, or minutes. He couldn't tell.

He couldn't fall asleep. Couldn't relieve himself. Couldn't even blasted sit.

He jumped when he heard a distant sound like a cart rolling. Hope flashed through him. Maybe someone was coming for him. A few minutes later, the door creaked noisily above him.

Light bobbed down the stairs. Blessed light.

One of the men was back, his face illuminated eerily by the dim glow. Hope died. The man removed the gag and Joran shifted his jaw, trying to loosen it, though it screamed in pain.

The man held up a cup , but Joran was suspicious enough to pull back. If it was going to knock him out again, he at least needed answers first.

"What are you going to do to me?" he began.

"Got word that you're the Prince of Ethereal. Just gonna keep you here until we can get a message to your father."

"I'm being ransomed?"

"Hopefully," the man laughed mirthlessly.

"Why?"

"Why not? The master knows a good opportunity when he sees one."

"Who is your master?"

"You'll meet him soon. Now, stop talking."

The man chuckled again and shoved the water to Joran's lips.

"We've got to take good care of you until we get our bargain," he sneered.

Joran swallowed the water. He'd need strength. It was frigid down there, and it looked like he would be standing for a long time.

The man also gave him a few bites of bread, which he forced himself to eat, though his stomach rebelled.

"We'll check on ya' in the morning, then. Guess there's no need for this," the man said, tossing the gag down. "No one would hear ya' way out here anyway. Good night!"

***

The night was worse than any misery Joran had been through. Pain raked through his shoulders until he cried out. Finally they went numb, which was almost worse. He shook from shock and exhaustion and fear, but he had to stay upright. If he lost his footing, he'd pull his wrists out of joint. Or crack them. The darkness continued to play tricks on him, and the cold enveloped him, wracking his body with shivers.

There was a window where the wall rose to just above ground level, and eventually there was enough thin light for him to make out the perimeters of the dank space. The cellar was wider than he'd thought, but the walls were hard-packed dirt, and the air was thick with the smell of wet and rot. Still, the pre-dawn brightening had never been so welcome.

When the door opened, he willed his numb, heavy body to respond and look up.

Life came rushing back into him when he saw who was there.

It was Petra.

***

Pity shone in her eyes as she took him in. She had no business feeling sorry for him. She was the reason —

"You did this," he snarled.

She met his gaze calmly, then bent to set her candle and a tray down on the floor. Joran hadn't noticed it at first, but there was a cup of tea on the tray. Steam rose from it, and his stomach tightened with longing.

"I know you have no reason to trust me," she said slowly. She glanced up the stairs and lowered her voice. "I'm sorry, Joran. For everything."

"Sorry?" he choked on the word, the tea forgotten. "Sorry is nothing. You've been one lie after another, one bag full of lies." He punctuated the statement with a crude curse. "What in the kingdom did you think you'd gain by pretending to guard me, only to sell me to kidnappers?"

"Please. Be quiet. Drink this." She held the hot tea to his lips and he didn't refuse. It slipped down his chin as he drank. It was warm and comforting, and felt heavenly pouring down his throat.

"Joran, please believe me when I say that not everything is as it seems."

He was cold and tired, but he tried to focus on her words.

"I'll never be able to believe anything you say."

Her lips thinned. "It may look like I'm working for these men, Joran, but I am just trying to make sure no one gets hurt. My loyalty will always belong to you."

"You used me, Petra."

"I protected you. Prince." She whispered tightly.

"If you had wanted to protect me, you would have warned me. Bringing me tea as I practically hang here waiting to be killed isn't the definition of protection."

"I didn't know anything about this until last night. Even if I'd been able to tell you, you don't trust me. You wouldn't have believed me." She raised a fine brow.

There was noise upstairs.

Petra retrieved the tray and cup and fled up the stairs. Joran heard the door close softly behind her and the latch fall into place.

CHAPTER TWENTY-TWO

Not many minutes later, the door opened again. One of the men from last night descended the rough stairs with someone Joran hadn't seen before. The second man was well-dressed, his shirt tucked around a thickening gut, and his shoulders were wide and strong.

He peered closely at Joran as if inspecting him.

"What is your name?" He rumbled.

"Joran Rearevgard," Joran mumbled.

The man continued to question him, circling him as he spoke. Joran felt like a piece of meat strung up.

Finally the man shrugged. "You appear to be the real thing." He narrowed his eyes at Joran. "Do you have any proof on you, boy? Something of the King's?"

Joran shook his head, and the man narrowed his eyes. "If you're lying, you'll pay with your life. A dead prince is just as much a statement as a hostage one. Kahr, let his hands down. That's unnecessary."

The man called Kahr cut his hands loose from the hook above his head. Joran's wrists were still knotted together and they fell limply. His hands and fingers had no feeling; he couldn't move them.

"Lock and bar the door behind us," the man in charge instructed as they left.

As the blood rushed back into his arms, pain followed. Spirits. He bit his lip to keep from crying out. His tired legs shook and he sank to the floor, exhaustion pulling him down into a coma of sleep.

The next thing he knew, there was a knocking on the window. He heard it in his sleep, and it went on for what seemed like a full minute before he differentiated it from his dream and pulled himself into consciousness.

He grimaced as he looked around for the sound. His neck was incredibly stiff. A shadow hovering over the dirty window caught his attention. The tapping sounded again, and he could see the shadow of a fist hitting the foggy glass. The light filtering through still had an early morning tinge.

He struggled up, crawling closer to the square pane. His ankles were also still tied together.

"Can you hear me, Joran?"

The voice pricked his heart with hope. It was the Captain.

"I'm here. I hear you," he said eagerly.

"We're surrounding the house now. There's an empty cart in front. How many people are inside, do you know?"

"Three, maybe four." *Or five, if Petra is on their side.*

"Are you bound?"

"Yes."

The Captain's voice was low and rough. "We're coming for you, Joran. Stay alive."

The shadow moved away from the window. Joran felt both hopeful and afraid. He wanted to call the Captain back, ask him to stay. He sat, struggling to reach the ropes on his ankles so he could try to untie them.

There was noise above. Someone was hurrying down the stairs. Petra came into view. She tripped on the last stair and winced when her knees hit the ground, but she scrambled over to Joran, throwing herself at his ropes and working frantically to loosen them.

"I tried to alert the city guard last night, but I couldn't get away for long. I was praying the message would reach them and they would find us here."

His ankles were free and she was kneeling in front of him, grunting as she worked to loosen the knot around his wrists. "It's an ambush, Joran. They plan to capture the Captain too."

"Wait. How did you 'get away' to serve me tea this morning?" He asked doubtfully.

"I made them tea first, but with a bit of their own concoction, the one that knocked you out. There wasn't enough to last a long time, so I couldn't make it back to the ship. I sent a message to the city guard with the first person I saw, then I rushed back here. The men last night said they would lure the crew here. I heard them planning the ambush. They had people hidden in the woods. We need to help!"

The rope finally fell, and he held his arms out, inspecting them. "Still attractive enough," he muttered, unable to hide his smirk when Petra's eyes widened.

She stood, ready to rush back up the stairs, but Joran was wary to follow her, even if she'd just untied him.

"If you got away to send a message Petra, why did you come back?" She looked desperate to hurry away, but he had to know.

"I was afraid they would move you somewhere else or even hurt you if they realized I was gone. I needed to be here, with you."

"And when they found out you drugged them?" He still had too many questions, although he made a move toward the stairs.

"I claimed it was an accident. I'd simply used the towel they smothered you with, to dry the cups before I poured the tea - how could I have known it was the towel with the poison on it?"

The door above them opened again. It was the leader this time. He glared at them. A knife glinted at his side.

Shouts filtered down from above. There were definitely more men now than the three men Joran had seen at his capture.

The man on the stairs threw the knife like a dagger. Joran jerked back, and the blade zinged past his chest. He didn't hesitate to grab the knife from where it bounced to the floor after hitting the wall, but the man had more weapons. He pulled a dagger and stalked closer. He didn't move his eyes from Joran's face. "Someone alerted the city guard," he growled. "If we can't have you to negotiate, they can't have you alive."

He and Joran were bent down low, each poised to strike. Petra sidestepped carefully. The man caught her tiny movement and whirled on her, slamming his blade into her before she had a chance to react. She stumbled to the floor.

Joran lunged, but the man had already spun to meet him. He slammed his fist into Joran's shoulder and the knife he gripped went flying. His muscles were stiff and his arms were still weak.

The man grabbed his collar and threw him backwards. Joran hit the floor, the wind rushing out of him. He gasped, fighting for air that wouldn't come.

He saw the man tear the dagger out of Petra's side. Blood ran down the blade as he aimed it again at Joran. Then something hit the man from behind and he stumbled, caught by surprise. Joran clawed his way to a sitting position, gulping in oxygen as he tried to see past the man's thick form.

Johnny had thrown himself onto the man's back and was hanging on for dear life around the man's neck. The man still held the dagger, and he aimed it behind him, bringing it down hard. The sailor roared, one arm coming loose, though he still held on with his other arm. Joran felt the adrenaline of a fight coursing through his veins, giving him strength. He knew how to bring a man down.

He watched for two more seconds, analyzing the big man's weakest point before throwing himself into the tussle. His punches were perfectly timed. Perfect hits. The tide turned and Joran and the crew member brought the man down together.

Joran grabbed the ropes that had held him captive just moments before and tied them deftly around the man's hands. The sailor nodded quickly to Joran, then ran up the stairs, tossing words over his shoulder. The only one Joran caught was, "Ambush."

Only then did Joran turn to Petra. She was in a puddle of blood. He felt icy daggers shoot through him.

She blinked, her black eyes clouded with pain, before twisting her head to see what had happened. The movement made her grimace.

"Don't move," Joran commanded. He ripped off his shirt, shoving it around her.

She hissed when he pushed it under her, her white skin turning even whiter, but he didn't stop until he had tied it around her middle as tightly as he dared. It was immediately soaked through.

She was bleeding out. He shoved his hands against the wound, her warm blood oozing between his fingers. Her shriek died off as her head slumped, the pain taking her consciousness.

"Spirits, will someone help me?!" he yelled.

The only answer he got was Kahr. The accomplice flew down the stairs and yanked Joran away from Petra.

"No! Stop, don't. She needs help," Joran yelled, but Kahr shoved the tip of a blade against his back. He felt the point already catching in his skin.

"Move with me, or you die," Kahr hissed.

Joran stumbled forward, tears catching in his throat. Petra was dying. Dying trying to save him. Dying under the ground next to the miscreant who was stirring from his own unconsciousness.

He felt vomit coming up. Kahr didn't stop even when Joran threw up, just shoved him out the back of the house. His vision was blurry, but he was surprised at the number of men he didn't recognize involved in the scuffle.

Kahr herded him to the treeline and no one stopped them. Joran tripped through the woods for a few yards, only to find that the trees opened again, this time on a small beach. He'd had no idea they were this close to the water. The beach was secluded.

A small rowboat waited, tied to a tree. Kahr pushed him toward the boat. Joran's boots splashed in the water, and he planted his feet. He wouldn't go with this man. If Kahr thought he could get away with a hostage, he was wrong.

But Kahr grabbed his neck and pushed Joran face down in the water before he had a chance to resist.

Salty water shot up his nostrils. He choked, only bringing in more water. He flailed, kicking his arms and legs, but the hand on his neck was like iron, and he couldn't get his head up out of the water.

He fought the rising panic. His eyes and nose and lungs burned, but he forced himself to go still. His head felt like it would burst but he let the tension drop from his muscles, going limp. Satisfied, Kahr finally let go, grabbing him by his waistband to haul him to the boat. Joran shoved up, not stopping to fill his lungs before he whirled on the man, his knuckles connecting with his abductor's nose so hard his arm throbbed.

Joran didn't let up, letting his fists fly until they were slipping on the blood pouring from the man's face. Kahr finally dropped and Joran let him go, struggling over to the rope that moored the rowboat. He used it to tie the man up as best as he could before he sprinted back toward the house.

***

A few hours later, Joran fell into his hammock on the Pearl. The physician had looked him over, but all he had was bruises. Others were more seriously injured. Kirk had a slash across his forehead, which was deep enough that it needed to be sewn shut. One man had a snapped wrist. And Petra had been stabbed.

But she was alive. The physician said it was a side wound. Nothing vital had been impacted. The ship's physician stitched her up and gave her something for the pain. She was resting in Kirk's cabin.

Joran had pieced together most of the story now. Maniv had been outside helping start the bonfire for Night of Fire when he noticed a cart. He wouldn't have thought anything of it passing by on the dark road, had he not recognized Petra in the back. There wasn't enough time to go back inside to alert the Captain, so he'd trailed them himself. The further out in the country they went, following no apparent path, the more he knew something wasn't right. He kept following them right up to the secluded, abandoned house. He'd watched them push Petra inside, her wrists bound.

Satisfied the kidnappers were going to be there overnight, and seeing only three men, Maniv rushed back to Emberton, where the feast was winding down. It was past midnight, and the crew was preparing to leave when they realized that Maniv, Joran, and Petra were missing. Maniv shared his story with them and they rushed back to the ship for weapons. When they arrived at the Pearl, the Captain found a hostage note waiting for him, asking him to come alone at dawn. Maniv plotted that if they arrived before sunrise, they could take the kidnappers by surprise and rescue Joran and Petra, so they set out. The directions on the note were hard to follow, and Maniv got lost several times as he tried to find the way back to the old country house.

When they arrived, shortly after dawn, they had been surprised at the ambush waiting for them in the woods that surrounded the house. The crew was outnumbered. Had the city guard not showed up around the same time, they would have been defeated.

"Petra told me she snuck out to call the city guard last night. She'd overheard the ambush plans," Joran volunteered, his voice flat. There was still more he wanted to ask Petra about later but at present he was too exhausted.

"We owe her our lives then," Captain Markus said heavily. "For now, the city guard is holding the men who abducted the Prince. We don't know who they are or entirely what their motives were, but I'll be part of the interrogation to find out. That's later. For now, we recuperate." He sent the men away with instructions to rest.

Everyone turned away, weary, but the Captain touched Joran's arm, stopping him.

"I've sent a message to your father about the incident, Joran." He sighed. "I just pray it reaches him before he has a chance to worry. I'm not sure if the kidnappers sent their own missive before we got there."

He peered at Joran, his eyes burning into him. "I almost failed him, Joran. Failed you. I'm sorry."

Joran didn't know what to say. This wasn't the Captain's fault. Spirits, the Captain had planned a desperate rescue to save him. He shook his head.

"There are things I regret deeply, Joran. I asked my family to sail with me when I first became a captain. They made my ship their home until we were ambushed while attacking an enemy ship. They died that night. I lost my beautiful wife and my two little boys because I was selfish enough to want them near me."

Joran shook his head again. Why was the Captain telling him this?

"I lost my ship too. I couldn't forgive myself. I was so angry. Until one day... One day I realized I was still alive, and I had to make a choice about how I would live the rest of my life. I chose to be thankful. I don't know if asking them to live aboard ship was a foolish decision or not, but I do know that for those seven years, I had everything I wanted. I had the people I loved most right beside me every day. Even if they were still alive now, the time I would have spent with them would be minimal compared to what we had. A captain is rarely on land, and even less on his own land. The One gave me seven full years with them."

Joran swallowed. He heard the tremor in the Captain's voice as he continued. "When I got this ship and returned to sea, I named it the Pearl to remind me of the lesson I heard many years ago. I was able to live again, even with the pain, because I had learned to be thankful for the time we had. But, Joran, if I lost you, I do not know if I could forgive myself again. Your father entrusted you to me, and he is my best friend. I would rather die than let him down."

"You're King Henry's friend?" Joran faltered.

"We were like brothers when we were younger."

"But you're Terindian."

"As a protectorate of Ethereal, Terind has always been closely aligned with your kingdom. When I was your age, both Terindian and Etherealan young men were trained at the Academy. Henry and I grew up together and trained together. We pledged to protect each other and care for each other's families if the need ever arose. He became King and I stayed in the military. After I lost my family, I lost touch with a lot of people, your father being one of them. I left behind my life on land, and let the sea have me. So, when Henry wrote to tell me he was giving me his son for a while, I was…surprised. Honored. Grateful."

"For me?" Joran was doubtful.

"For you, for the chance to get to know the son of my long-ago friend. Grateful for the chance to be trusted by your father, even after I neglected our friendship. I praise the One for not letting me lose you tonight. I couldn't take another loss like that."

He patted Joran's shoulder gruffly and walked toward his cabin.

***

Joran fell into a deep sleep.

He woke in the dark, trying to get his bearings. It appeared to be the middle of the night. Something had woken him. He listened in the dark, but heard nothing except the breathing of the other men and the soft lap of water against the hull of the ship.

Still, his nerves were prickling. He sat up slowly, expecting something to hurl at him from the shadows.

He grit his teeth. Everything hurt. Again.

Then his eyes caught a soft glow from the hatch, then a shadow, then nothing. Someone was going above deck, which was nothing to be alarmed about. Still, he couldn't shake the eerie feeling. He felt his way to the stairs, easing open the door at the top. The moon shone brightly, casting the deck in grayscale, like a moment frozen in time. He let his lungs swell as he breathed in the crisp, cold air.

A movement caught the corner of his vision.

Someone was hunched down, creeping toward the main cabins. The watchman on the other side of the deck wouldn't be able to see whoever it was.

The figure paused at the door of Kirk's cabin. Dread ballooned in Joran's gut as he watched the person open the door and slip inside.

He paused for the briefest second. He wanted to grab his sword, but it was below deck. Instinct told him he couldn't waste time. He sprinted to the cabin and flung open the door.

Moonlight spread into the small room. Maniv spun toward him from where he had been bent over the bunk. Over Petra.

The cook didn't hesitate. He rushed at Joran, who barely had time to steady himself to catch the impact. The man was armed, and his knife flashed dangerously in the soft light.

Petra garbled something from the bunk, but Joran was too focused on Maniv to hear her.

He ducked as Maniv slashed at his neck.

"What in the name of the spirits are you doing in here?" Joran demanded.

Maniv merely hissed, sidestepping a blow and striking again before Joran could recover his stance. The blade swiped across Joran's arm, leaving a burning path behind. He let out a cry, but didn't look away.

"What were you going to do to her? Kill her?" He shouted again.

Maniv stumbled into a stool and Joran took the moment of recovery to strike. He grabbed Maniv's wrist while simultaneously kneeing him in the gut. The cook gasped as his air left him. Joran bent the man's wrist until he howled.

Footsteps pounded on deck, mingling with the anguished scream from Maniv's throat.

The watchman was there. Captain Markus was there. Two other sailors appeared just a few seconds behind them.

"Hold him," Joran panted. The night guard jumped into action, helping Joran tie the man up. "He was going to stab Petra."

Maniv glared at them from the floor.

Joran wanted to kick him again, but he stepped away instead.

Petra was watching them with wide eyes. "He must be the kidnapper's contact on the Pearl. I knew it must be someone. I didn't know who they had contact with on our ship." Her voice was thick and sluggish, and her words didn't make sense.

Captain Markus towered over Maniv and glared down at him. "Take him to my quarters, so I can speak with him."

The sailors heaved Maniv away.

"Thank you," Petra slurred. The pain medicine was making her groggy.

Captain Markus looked at Joran. "Do you think he planned to kill her?"

"She'd be dead if I had been two seconds later," Joran confirmed, no pride in his tone.

"I'll get to the bottom of this," Captain Markus promised. "Petra, I'll have someone I trust stand guard outside your door tonight."

"I'll do it," Joran volunteered.

The Captain raised his bushy eyebrows. "Are you up to it, Joran?" He looked pointedly at the slash on Joran's arm.

"Yes, sir." The cut wasn't deep. There was no way he'd be able to go back to sleep right now anyway.

Petra smiled sloppily and waved her fingertips at them. "You're so nice," she whispered.

Joran's cheeks pinkened in the dark, entirely for her sake. She'd hate knowing how drunk she sounded right now.

He nodded to her and slipped out the door.

***

Two days passed before Petra was able to lessen her pain medication and stop acting like a fool. Joran felt the soreness in his limbs beginning to ebb, and the Captain informed him that the interrogation would happen that afternoon.

Maniv had joined the others in the holding cells in the city, now in the custody of the city's guard. He had admitted to being part of the band of men who had taken Joran. He was planted on the Pearl to feed the Captain false tips to keep him from finding their raids or their smuggling vessels. He'd told his master that the Prince was on board and helped them plan the abduction. The story of him following the cart and his idea to take the crew for a surprise attack had all been part of the plan. He'd wanted to destroy Petra before the trial so she couldn't testify against the rest of the men. She'd heard too much, and she was supposed to have been killed already.

Joran knocked on Petra's cabin door.

"Come in," she called. Her voice was clear and normal.

He ducked into the doorway. "Hello," he said. He glanced around, suddenly unsure.

Petra gave him a half-smile. "I'm sitting up. Doc says he wants me to start walking by tomorrow, but spirits, it's tough to get out of bed."

"You should take your time," Joran offered.

"Perhaps, but I think the physician is right. He said I need the blood to flow. Movement will help me heal faster."

They were quiet.

"Thank you for saving my life," she finally said.

Joran shrugged. "A life for a life." He tried to sound casual.

"Except you saved mine three times now."

Joran grinned. "I don't think that's how this guard thing is supposed to work. I may need to start looking for new protection."

"I definitely owe you," she grinned back and then sobered. "Has the Captain said anything…about me?"

Joran perched on the stool and studied Petra. She was different. And the same. It still unnerved him a bit.

"The Captain hasn't, but Petra, I don't know if... I don't think you can be my guard anymore."

She turned her fathomless eyes on his, the way she had done every time before she said something sensible, something that maddened Joran because it was always something *true*, but he didn't want to hear it. "I understand. But I want you to know, I'm the same person, Joran."

His jaw dropped. "But you're not. You were Peter and I thought of you as a friend. I trusted you with a lot of things about myself that I never would have shared with anyone, but you acted a part for me every single day. You're not that person. You're, you're..." he threw his palms up helplessly. How could he explain it?

"I'm Petra. And I'm still your friend, the one who listened to you."

He shifted uncomfortably, and she changed the subject.

"The interrogation is soon?"

"This afternoon."

"Joran, Maniv is the one who sold you to those men."

"I wish you would have said that earlier – before he tried to kill you. He admitted as much to the Captain,

Of Oceans and Pearls

and he's locked up with the rest of them. But I'd like to hear the rest of the story if you're able to tell me now."

"There were several things I didn't put together until after he attacked me. Now I think I should have realized there was something suspicious about him a long time ago. Every time I worked with him, he asked me questions, mostly about you. I thought he was just talkative, but he must have been fishing for information. It wasn't suspicious enough to raise any alarms until the night of the storm. I stayed below when it first hit, trying to stay calm. He came downstairs and rummaged through your bag. He didn't see me in the shadows and I didn't stop him because I wanted to see what he was after. He eventually left without finding anything, from what I could see. I went on the top deck then, trying to find you. I assumed you'd sent him to fetch something and thought I could help...that's when everything else happened." She tucked her hair behind her ears. Joran willed himself to stay quiet, although questions were burning his throat.

"The night of the feast, I lagged behind you all. The Captain told me I was welcome to come along, but I no longer felt like part of the crew, so I kept my distance. I was far enough behind that no one noticed when a pair of men, who had been following us from a distance, caught up with me and grabbed me."

"They knew I was your guard. They told me they needed me to lure you outside sometime during the feast – alone. They took my weapons and said they'd be watching me closely to make sure I obeyed. If I talked to anyone else beside you, or did anything suspicious, they would harm the Captain. One of them showed me a small bottle, which he said held poison. I saw that same man at the feast. He hovered near the Captain the whole time, silently reminding me what was at stake."

"Of course I tried to find out who they were and what their plans were, but I couldn't gather any names, just the fact that the 'master' they worked for planned to kill you as a statement to the King. They said something about your father ruining their trade business. I told them you were your father's favorite and that they would have much better results, if they used you to bargain with him for whatever they wanted."

"When I awoke in the cart, you weren't there."

"They tied me up and handed me over to their master. I was in his cart, which left several minutes after yours. When we got to the old house, I didn't know where you were, and I was terrified they had already killed you, until I saw them go down to the cellar. They spoke freely in front of me, probably because they planned to kill me before morning. I heard them say they had a man on every ship in the Bristian Ocean, but I didn't have time to wonder about it because then they began talking about the note they'd left for the Captain, and the other plan they'd concocted to confuse him. I heard them say that 'all their men were getting in place,' and that they expected the whole crew before dawn. 'We can get rid of them in one swipe. No one will find the bodies out here,' the master said. I realized they were planning an ambush and I needed to get help. I offered to make them tea, so they untied me, and I drugged them. Then I ran back in the direction of the town, trying hard to leave a trail. I stopped at the first house I saw, woke the family, and begged them to ride into the city and send the guard after me. I hoped and prayed they would believe me, and they seemed concerned and agreed to help. I told them which direction to send the guard, promising the trail would be marked. I followed my own trail back and was able to check on you before they awoke. It wasn't until Maniv tried to attack me here on the ship, that it started to make sense."

She finally clamped her mouth shut and Joran sighed. She really had tried her best to make sure everyone was safe.

"And, Joran? There's one more thing. I haven't told the Captain. When I was down there in that cellar with the man they called their master – after I came to, and you were gone –" she paused to lick her lips nervously.

"I saw his hand, uh, fall off. I guess the ropes had loosened it. He managed to secure the straps well enough to hold it on his wrist, but it wasn't a real hand. He's missing his left hand. I thought you should know."

Joran felt like all the air had been sucked out of his lungs.

***

He'd pleaded with the Captain to let him go that afternoon. He needed to be there. If that man was the Left-Handed...he grit his teeth together.

Joran and Kirk were told to wait outside. Only Captain Markus was allowed in the building. Kirk leaned against the building and complained about the cold, but Joran's insides were too hot to notice it.

An hour later, the Captain finally reappeared.

Joran rushed up to him, trying to keep his voice under control. "I need to speak with that man," he said. "I need to find out something for myself."

He didn't wait for a response, just pushed into the building and toward the interrogation cells. The man was chained, but he looked unharmed. Joran glared at his unmarred face. He wanted to beat it bloody.

"Put up your hands," he demanded, rushing into the cell before the guards closed the door. The Captain was on his heels, but Joran ignored him.

The man's gaze flickered from Joran to the Captain and back, but he raised his hands. Joran lunged at his left hand, gripping the realistic-looking wax and pulling it off. Hidden straps slid out of the man's sleeve.

Something like amusement sparked in the man's eyes, but Joran couldn't focus on anything but the roaring in his head. He flew at the man, pounding his fists into him. The chains kept the assassin from being able to hit him back and Joran took advantage of the free reign, pummeling the man's face.

"Joran!" The Captain's sharp voice bled into his raging fury, but he didn't slow until he was yanked backward.

He stumbled back, breathing hard, glaring at the man in chains. "You killed my bride," he choked. "You killed her!" He was screaming, and he couldn't stop.

Captain Markus shook him. Guards surrounded him.

He backed up.

"Joran, get a hold of yourself," the Captain demanded. "What are you talking about?"

Joran turned his glare on the Captain. "He's the Left-Handed. He assassinated my fiancée two years ago. He needs to die."

The Captain gripped Joran's shoulders. "The man is wicked but he's not the Left-Handed. He's actually his rival. The man you just bloodied is Felix Bagden. Several years ago he survived an assassination attempt from that man and lost his hand, but got away with his life. He deserves worse than you gave him, I agree, but it's not your place to do it. Now, that's enough. Go," and he was pushed toward the exit.

Once outside, he broke away from the Captain's grip and fled.

CHAPTER TWENTY-THREE

Joran ran blindly, half expecting Kirk to come running after him to drag him back to Captain Markus. But maybe the Captain knew he needed to be alone for a while. When no one stopped him, he slowed. He wandered the streets for the rest of the day, letting his anger seep out. Despair crept into its place.

He didn't know what had happened to Krynn, not really. He'd assumed her killer was the infamous assassin they were chasing, but there was no way to prove it. He'd felt so close to some semblance of closure in that room just now, only to find he'd attacked the wrong man. Maybe. Maybe it was him, somehow, but again, he'd never really know. And bloodying the man's face hadn't helped the way he imagined. Like the night he'd stabbed Avalon, the lost princess from Haven. He'd expected that making his mother feel her loss the way she had made him feel Krynn's would somehow make up for it, but it hadn't. Avalon had lived. A healer had saved her before it was too late, and he was glad now that he didn't have her death on his conscience too. He could hardly believe he'd stooped so low.

He felt for Krynn's ring absentmindedly. His thumb touched skin.

His eyes jerked to his hand. His finger was bare. The ring was gone.

He blinked at the empty space in disbelief then scoured the ground around him as though it had just fallen off, but the truth was, he wasn't sure how long it had been gone.

It was too much. How could he take anymore? His life had started falling apart the day his birdie died and things were still crumbling around him.

He turned into the town, pulling out the coins he had left from his pay, the ones he hadn't spent on a silly pearl. The kidnappers hadn't been common thieves, as everything in his pockets remained. The jacin he'd won the day before they took him had been ruined by his dunking underwater, but he was pretty sure he could find more in this city. They'd caught Felix Bagden, leader of one of the biggest crime syndicates in Kerrynth, and he hardly cared. He was supposed to be helping Captain Markus catch drug suppliers, but he was a fake. He hated jacin, but he needed it, and today he couldn't stop himself. He was tired of fighting.

Of Oceans and Pearls

It began to rain as he headed west, out of Hollowsprit. He didn't know where he was heading, but he kept walking until he crested a rise. Land splayed out below him, and he felt high and removed, the way a bird must feel as it peers down at the earth.

It was raining hard, but he didn't move. Somewhere out there, Krynn was buried. Her letters were erased. Her ring was gone. He had lost her, and now he'd lost everything he'd had of her.

You still have the memories, a voice reminded him, but he ignored it.

He couldn't find her killer. He couldn't avenge her death. His mother was dead, his father hated him, and he was sure he had pushed Captain Markus to his limit by now too. No one would keep trusting him over and over, letting him come back again and again. And then there was Petra, who had thrown his life all off balance again. He couldn't reconcile her goodness with her deceit. He couldn't reconcile her with Peter, the friend he'd grown to...love.

He fisted the fresh jacin in his pocket, drawing it out and shielding it from the rain. He let the powder fly up his nostrils as he inhaled, exhaling the breath through his mouth. He did it several times, basking in the warm headiness that followed.

For the first time in months, he was able to forget. Forget everything. The storm had matured and lightning pierced through the sky. He grinned up at it and raised a fist to Heaven. *Pour, One, flood me. Drown me. Try it.*

He smirked. He was invincible.

***

He woke up slowly. Everything was cloudy. He tried to see, but couldn't and it scared him. He felt a strong dark current pulling him and he couldn't fight it. He closed his eyes, letting it pull him down.

The voices continued, finally plunging through his subconscious again and bringing him to the surface.

Everything was wet. He was floating.

"He's awake."

He recognized the voice. Calm and low. He blinked. Drops of water were falling on his face, making it hard to see.

His head hurt.

Petra was there.

Spirits, a bunch of people were there. He squinted.

"I didn't know if I could bring you back, boy," a man's voice said near his head. A stranger was kneeling over him. "You took so much of that wicked stuff that it nearly took you."

Things came filtering back slowly. He eased up on his elbow. He wasn't sure why he was lying on the ground in the rain, but he felt sheepish. He'd run. Drugs. He'd felt so good. He remembered that part, the lightness in his chest. More drugs.

He peered up again. Captain Markus, Kirk, Serb, Petra. They all stared back, drenched in the rain.

And no one looked angry. He studied their faces in the dark and wondered if he was seeing things from the jacin. Petra looked stricken with relief. The Captain looked concerned. Kirk looked almost…soft. Like he was close to crying. Serb was grinning.

The doctor wrapped his arm around his back and helped him sit up.

"What happened?" Joran asked.

"You ran away. I expected you to run off some of your steam and return, but when it got dark and you hadn't returned, I knew we had to look for you," the Captain said.

"Why?"

"You're part of my crew. My family. No one had any idea where you might have gone. We wandered around town for a while, asking around, but no one had noticed you. I returned to the ship when the storm hit. Petra begged me to go back out, and she was determined to go with me."

Joran took in Petra. Her breathing was ragged, and she hunched slightly.

"You tried to come after me on foot, two days after you got stabbed?" He was incredulous.

She nodded.

"Petra, that's not what the doc meant by walking!" He cried.

She let out a soft laugh. "You certainly need a new guard then if you don't want me saving your life," she said, her voice wet with tears.

"She's the one who told us to head west. She knew you might be trying to get closer to Glensprit for some reason," Kirk volunteered.

Joran's throat swelled. "Thank you. All of you," he said huskily.

***

Joran was standing on the deck when someone came up beside him. He turned to see Petra.

Captain said they'd be casting off tomorrow. Petra wouldn't be going with them, would she? He hadn't found out yet, but he suddenly wanted to know.

She spoke first though. "Joran, I know you've struggled with accepting me, trusting me, but I said this before and I'll say it again: my loyalties have always been with you. If you ever feel like things are overwhelming, and the pain and anger are crushing you, please go to someone. The men on this ship? They care about you. They consider you family. And you can turn to me too. I'll be here. I'll be here to listen to all of it and help you handle it. With you. You don't have to face it alone. Please just don't put that stuff in your body ever again."

She turned to face him and he saw her eyes glistening.

"I promise," he said, and he meant it.

She turned her gaze back to the sea. "We're almost even now, with this life-saving thing," she smiled. "Let's not go on building the tally, though. A guard pledges his own life. Even an imposter one takes the pledge, and Joran? I meant it."

He looked down, rubbing at the missing ring out of habit.

"I lost it," he said suddenly. "Her ring." He held up his bare hand. "I don't know when."

"You had it at the tavern the night you started the brawl." She scrunched her face up at the sky. "I don't think I saw it after that."

"The storm," he said. He could still feel the water leaching at his life if he closed his eyes. "I probably lost it in the sea that night."

Petra's face sobered. "Then you lost it saving me."

His eyes met hers, and he held her gaze, a tangle of emotions constricting around his heart.

CHAPTER TWENTY-FOUR

Petra pulled something out of her pocket. "I kept this for you," she said. "I thought you might be ready for it at some point. Maybe this is what Maniv was looking for in your satchel."

She handed him a letter. He turned it over. It was the letter from his father, the one he had never opened. His heart lurched and he looked up quickly, but she had already walked away.

He fingered the corner of the letter. The water rolled gently below. He could let it go, right now, and send the message to a watery grave.

He sighed. He didn't really want to this time.

He found a corner by himself and broke the seal.

The letter was long, small words covering the length of two pages. His gaze flickered. This was his father's own handwriting, not the work of a scribe.

My son,

Of Oceans and Pearls

I've thought of you every day since you've left. I've never sent any of my sons so far away and it feels like part of me is missing. The Captain who agreed to take you, Captain Markus, has tried to keep me abreast of his route, but letters, especially from a sailing ship, are rare.

I hope you receive this one. It's time to tell you how I really feel.

The attack last month turned my world upside down, or perhaps I should say, righted it. I can't explain how shocking it was to finally become aware of life again. For years, I'd lived in a stupor, a darkness that I couldn't put my finger on, and I felt constantly confused and sure, all at the same time. I made terrible decisions during that time. I know about them now. Yet somehow, my kingdom remains, and the Great Magister, whose revolt helped free us all, has been gracious in helping me make right all the things that were wrong.

I failed you, Joran. Only now am I realizing how much I failed you. You could never come to me with problems or worries. People tell me it was difficult to have a decent conversation with me most of the time. You could not rely on me for help. You could not even trust me to save you from your mother's evil. I had let her magic overcome me, and I was powerless.

I have so many regrets. Benrid's blindness, inflicted by your mother. Your disgrace, furthered by your mother. Golan's shame of illegitimacy, hidden by your mother. My own downfall, the result of Lilian as well. But all of these things ultimately fall back on me. I should have known better. I knew Lilian was conniving, yet I let her have her way. I failed my sons. I hurt them.

And now it hurts me every day.

I regret her. But never do I regret my sons. I do not regret you, Joran.

I lashed out at you in a way a father should never treat a son, and I'm sorry. It wasn't you I found appalling that night – it was me. All I could see was how much I had hurt you, and I couldn't bear it.

Great Magister Erlich suggested you join a ship. He thought some time and space away from the castle would be good for you, for both of us, and that the discipline and tough way of life might help you mature. I agreed, but the real reason I sent you away, especially so hurriedly, was not because you were repulsive. It was because I felt unworthy to be your father. All I could see were my failures. I didn't want you to hurt for one more day because of me. I was desperate for someone, something, that could be better to you than I was. That could save you.

I love you, Joran. I don't know if I can ever ask you to love me back, after a lifetime of ignoring you, but I hope that one day you will forgive me.

You're free to choose your path. After your year of service is up, I'll respect any decision you make, but I want you to know that you will always have a place here, even if it's simply to be my son. I look forward to welcoming you home, if that's what you choose.

Your loving father,

Henry

Joran stared at the signature. Simple, informal. The King hadn't even added his title.

The words blurred through the veil of tears hovering in his eyes. He took a shuddering breath and tilted his head back against the wood.

The sky was bright and clear, all traces of yesterday's storm vanished. He stared into the blue above, as endless as the ocean itself.

"One?" He questioned. Petra prayed. She believed. He wasn't sure if he did, but he was willing to try. He licked his lips and tried again.

"Thank you."

He couldn't think of what else to say. All of it was still too tangled under the surface, but something calm settled in his heart. He hadn't felt that way for years.

***

Joran stayed in his corner for a long time, but he finally uncurled himself and went to find Petra.

She was in her cabin. She glanced at the unfolded pages in his hand and her eyes brightened with pleasure, though she didn't say anything.

"I read it." Joran waved the papers slightly. He sighed and fell onto the pile of coiled rope. "It was...surprising. My father, ah, asked me to forgive him." He swallowed, hoping his emotions wouldn't get the best of him again.

Petra perched on the edge of the bunk, intense, patient, calm. Just like always.

"So, how did you end up with this letter? I got rid of it at the tavern."

"You left it on the table. The serving woman was offended when you ignored her. She frowned at the letter and flounced away. I went to retrieve it because I didn't want you to regret it later. Then you decided to punch a man." She let out a low laugh. "I've had it since then. It just never felt like the right time until now."

Joran could only take so much emotion before brushing it off with humor. He smirked now. "Catren wasn't as interesting as I thought then, seeing as how you were still watching me."

Petra flushed. "Well, no. She – I..."

It was Joran's turn to flush. Right. Of course.

"Well, thanks," he mumbled lamely. "I don't think I would have accepted it before now. I'm glad you kept it. I should write a reply and send it before we cast off in the morning."

He didn't move.

"Are you, will you – be coming with us?" He fumbled.

A smile whispered over her lips. "Yes, for now. Captain Markus said I can have this cabin. Poor Kirk, ousted to the smelly bunk room. But it will only be for about a month or a bit more. Captain plans to return to Kestell after the Smyer Isles. I'll get off there and report to Magister Erlich and King Henry and then return to my grandfather."

Happiness and disappointment warred in Joran's chest. She would stay with them. But only for a few more weeks.

"What will I do for a guard?" He quirked an eyebrow, but it didn't hide the huskiness in his voice.

Her lips twitched. "I think you'll be fine. I needed one more than you did." She tossed her hand in a wide circle. "You've got a good family here on board. You all will watch out for each other."

He nodded. "You're not afraid of going back to your grandfather? You told the Captain you were in the beginning."

Petra smiled wider. "He wrote to me. I got the letter when you got yours in Bristia. I'd written to him before I left Ethereal, explaining why I'd disappeared after the secret mission. I also told him about becoming your guard. I wanted him to know what had happened, but I didn't expect anything from him. His letter took a while to reach us, but he wrote it as soon as he received mine. He told me he loved me and that nothing I could do would change that love because I was his granddaughter. His love isn't based on what I do, but who I am, and I will always be his. He told me I could never be in the military again, but he would pardon me for deserting, based on the circumstances of the men threatening my life, and that I would always be welcome in his home." Her face was practically glowing and Joran's chest tightened.

He watched her tuck her hair behind her ears. She glanced at him self-consciously. "Cutting my hair was the hardest thing," she admitted. "Hiding my, ah, self didn't matter, and getting up before everyone to use the privacies was a small nuisance, but cutting my hair? I cried the whole time." She shrugged, as if it was nothing now.

Then it hit him. He flinched like he had been punched in the gut. She had done it for him. All this time, he had focused on the way she had lied to him, betrayed him by pretending to be someone she wasn't, but she hadn't done it to him at all. She had done it *for* him. She had sacrificed her identity for him, left her beautiful curtain of hair lying on a floor somewhere, and abandoned her only relative, all for his well-being.

Spirits, she had boarded a blasted ship and gone to sea when she couldn't even swim. He blinked rapidly. How many times had he taken out his twisted feelings on her, scorning her and ridiculing? And how many times had he let his grief gush out, the memories he'd kept locked away for so long, drowning her with a flood of his own problems? And she had always listened, even though she had enough of her own hurts to drown in.

He remembered the bite in her words when she had looked at him and explained that her little sister had been gifted. She told them how Lia had tried to fly too far over the pond, her eyes flashing at him defensively like he had doubted her story before. The truth was, he had never questioned how a six year old girl had gotten so far into the water that her big sister couldn't fish her out even if she couldn't swim. He hadn't cared enough to think about it.

Everything she did, she did for others. She'd risked her life with the rogue soldiers in Cleft, playing spy among them, all for the sake of gifted people she didn't even know. Spirits, while he'd been trying to kill Avalon, Petra was risking her life to save gifted people like the Princess.

She was good. So very *good* and selfless.

And beautiful.

"Your hair will grow," he said, voice deep. "But I'm sure it won't make you any more stunning than you are now."

Her eyes flickered in surprise.

He felt dumb.

"I should go find a pen and paper," he concluded lamely, indicating the letter he still held.

Petra nodded.

CHAPTER TWENTY-FIVE

Joran finished writing the letter for his father. He found Captain Markus to ask permission to leave and post it.

The Captain smiled broadly when he saw the address. "Of course, Joran. May it travel with speed. I'm sure your father is yearning for it."

Joran turned, then paused. "Captain?" he said. He met the Captain's fierce eyes, which were no longer as frightening as they used to be. "Thank you. You didn't have to come after me – either time, but I'm grateful you did." He took a breath.

"That means a lot to me, Prince Joran," Captain Markus said. "The men have helped you too. They would appreciate hearing your gratitude as well."

Joran thought of Kirk reeling him out of the water, Johnny attacking Felix Bagden from behind, and Tips calling him Stomper. He nodded. "I'll tell them."

Joran sent the letter, meandering his way back to the ship slowly. The late afternoon sun glowed warmly, though it didn't touch the chill in the air. When he finally rounded the corner to the harbor, the Pearl bobbed steadily against her mooring, a beacon of hope. He felt the warmth of familiarity, of home, fan in his chest. A few months ago, he'd been prodded up the gangplank against his will. This time he took the step off land by choice.

***

"Will you join me on deck tonight?" Joran asked Petra at dinner.

They had been sailing for a week and were still a few days from the Smyer Isles. Petra was moving almost normally. She was still exempt from the heavier duties, but her wound was healing well, despite the agony she had put herself through the night Joran had gone missing outside Hollowsprit.

She regarded him curiously.

He let his dimples show. "I hear the stars are spectacular here."

She lifted a brow. "Here? Really?"

He rolled his eyes. "Yes, the views at night from the middle of nowhere on the sea are better than anywhere else."

Petra smirked. "Then I'd love to see them."

Several hours later, Joran paced the deck impatiently. The night was deep black and clear. And cold. He stomped his feet, trying to keep the blood flowing.

There was shuffling. He looked up and caught his breath.

Petra stood before him in a long dress, the color of frozen lavender. The icy hue made her look spectral in the moonlight. He couldn't help dropping his eyes to take in her figure. She was tall and willowy, her curves alluring. How had she been able to conceal herself so well?

He blinked back his surprise and grinned, holding out an arm.

"Is this elegant woman Petra, or are you an apparition sent to taunt me?"

Petra looked uncomfortable. "I just…it's been a long time. Breeches are so practical, but I thought…tonight I wanted to feel…"

"Beautiful? Because you are," Joran said honestly.

The hint of a smile touched her face. "I was going to buy more paper in Hollowsprit for my sketching, but instead, I bought this."

"I'm glad. But it's too cold for phantom clothes," he said, draping a blanket around her.

He sat on a barrel and patted another beside him.

Maybe you're not angry with the girl. Maybe it's something else you're feeling, Kirk had said. He'd replayed the statement in his head endless times since then.

He chanced a glance at Petra, then squinted into the distance. He was feeling something. Love? He didn't know for sure yet, just that it was good. Solid. Real.

He cleared his throat and opened his mouth to say something, but Petra turned toward him suddenly. "I'm not her, Joran."

He blinked. Of course not. Petra wasn't anything like Krynn. Krynn had been perfect. He'd always love her, probably always miss her.

But Petra was perfect too.

"I don't want you to be her," he said softly. "I loved her a lot. She's not someone I'll ever be able to forget, but she's gone. And you came in and filled all the empty spaces. You're the beauty in all of my brokenness. I don't want you to be anything – anyone – except yourself. *Petra.*"

She nodded, her lips trembling ever so slightly.

He suddenly couldn't tear his gaze away from her mouth, from the dip in her full bottom lip. He laughed softly. "Spirits Petra, what have you done to me? Would you believe the first day we mended sails together, I looked at you and – I wanted to kiss you? I didn't understand it then." He shook his head.

She met his gaze with her serious eyes. "Would you believe, Joran, that I wanted to kiss you from the moment you tried to bolt off the river ship, right after you stepped foot on it?"

"Wait, really?"

"Really. It's not every day I get to wrestle an impossibly attractive man to the ground. What would you expect me to feel?" She smirked.

He exhaled with amusement. "Then I'm sorry I didn't give you any more opportunities to plow me down."

She rolled her eyes. "That time was enough. I was terrified you'd discover my secret right then, but you were too deep in your own pit of despair to notice anything," she scoffed.

"Well, it looks like we've both been waiting a long time," he whispered, lifting the pad of his thumb to caress the pouty dent in her lip.

His eyes met hers. "Shall we?"

Then he leaned in. She met him, and their lips crashed into each other, parting to pull each other in. Fire raced through his core and he wrapped an arm around her, pulling her against him. His other hand cupped her cheek, guiding her closer, his thumb stroking her cheekbone and then getting lost in her hair.

She darted her tongue against his lip and he groaned, his own tongue responding, tasting her bottom lip, pulling, needing. She was delicious.

"Petra." He breathed her name against her mouth, his breath mingling with hers in her pleased intake of air.

This kiss didn't feel like painful memories, the way he'd always felt when he kissed someone since Krynn. For the first time, it felt like tomorrow. Like hope.

When they finally pulled apart, Joran wasn't sure he wouldn't fall right back against those lips. His gaze was hooded as he raked her face with his eyes.

"You said the stars were beautiful out here," she reminded him, her voice thick.

"They are." He didn't take his eyes off her. "They're the most beautiful I've ever seen."

She smiled and turned to lie back against his chest. He put both arms around her, burying his face in her unruly strands of hair and breathing her in, pleased at the way she fit in his arms.

"The Captain told me he heard that the stars are on fire," he offered.

They looked up. Stars shimmered across the sky like powder from a shattered crystal.

"I've heard that the stars are a map," she said. "They create pictures to tell a story. You can also set your course toward one, and if you're lucky, you'll reach it and it will take you to another realm."

"I see a picture. A dragon's head. See that bright one? It's his demonic eye." His warm breath whispered across her neck, and he saw goosebumps rise.

He nuzzled his lips against the pricks of flesh and she reached back to twist her fingers gently in his hair.

CHAPTER TWENTY-SIX

A week later he emerged from the bunkroom before dawn, joining Petra at the rail, her gaze focused on the eastern sky. Land dotted the horizon, lit from behind by a soft-pink glow.

Petra leaned her head against his shoulder. "Thanks for coming. I know getting up early isn't something you enjoy."

He put his arm around her. "If my girl will watch the stars with me, I'll gladly watch the sunrise with her," he assured her.

"I know you haven't seen many of these," she teased, "So be prepared to be amazed."

He traced her ear with his fingertip. "I am, Petra. I'm amazed."

She twisted to meet his gaze as he traced her face with his eyes. She looked vulnerable in the thin light, untypical doubt clouding her eyes.

"I'm nothing, Joran. Other than my old noble name — and no family or wealth left to go behind it — I am nothing."

He furrowed his brows. "You're everything, Petra. Spirits, you're the reason I'm still alive to see this sunrise. But besides that, you were the first friend I've had in years. You were kind when I was rude, you were calm when I was angry, you were patient when I failed. You were loyal when I hated you and when I stopped trusting you. You were honest when I needed the truth. You were confident when I felt lost. You are everything to me."

He put his arms around her and pulled her against his chest. He felt her tremble as she released a breath. He tried to imagine the rest of his life without her by his side, the way she had been for the past few months, and, spirits, he couldn't. The thought of her not being with him was terrifying. And then he knew.

"Petra," he whispered down to her ear, his cheek still pressed against the top of her head. "I need you. I needed you since the day you knocked me down when I tried to jump ship, and I've only needed you more every day since. And I *want* you. Forever."

She didn't move and Joran's chest grew tight with anxiety. He'd lost before, but he couldn't lose again. Not like this. He loved her so much it hurt. Loved her intelligent eyes, her deadly level-stare, her subtle humor. He loved the way she could wield a sword and carry her weapons like a soldier. He loved her bravery and her honesty. He loved the way she listened. And cared. He loved her night-sea eyes and black, tousled hair.

"I've already pledged my loyalty to you, Joran."

His heart sank. "But I want you to marry me. I'm in love with you." His voice cracked desperately.

"And now I pledge my love," she finished simply, raising her serious eyes to his. He blinked in surprise before a grin split his face.

"I love every bit of who you are, Joran. I've been falling in love with you for months and I had to fight it down so many times. I never dreamed it could be anything beyond a secret in my heart."

"Me? Even when I was an idiot?"

Her lips twitched. "Especially then. I suppose you have no idea how handsome you are when you glower."

He kissed her then. Finally she pulled back and glanced at the sky. "Well, you've missed another sunrise, Your Highness."

He sighed.

"Which only means we'll have to do this again," she threatened, an eyebrow arched, and he groaned.

***

A few hours later, they sailed into the bay of the largest island of Smyer. The other islands were small and uninhabited, but Captain Markus said they would take their time searching them for hidden coves where the pirate ship may have taken cover.

Winter was setting in, the mountainous islands braving the icy wind from the Myah Sea. Ice fishing preparation was in full swing. The Smyer fishermen were getting ready to sail north to the Earth Kingdoms for the ice fishing season in Oceania, which began in several weeks.

"We need to assimilate here as quickly as possible," Captain Markus instructed his crew. "We're new here, and we're not a fishing vessel, which makes us stand out. If the Left-Handed is here, or if he has contacts in this town, he'll soon know about us. We can't alert him any more than necessary. We are here to inquire about brokering a business partnership for a merchant in Terind who is looking to invest their pearl harvests in the spring."

"Keep up the facade and stay alert. Try to listen and find out what you can."

The men nodded.

They spent the next three nights in taverns around the city, coaxing information out of drunk men.

Of Oceans and Pearls

Sitting around cozy fires and sipping ale, sheltered from the cold outside, was a pleasant way to spend the evenings. Joran slipped into his role with ease, holding sway over strangers with his humor and stories, though he glanced often at Petra, hoping to see her lips twitch. He showcased his charm and people opened up to him easily, talking without abandon.

Still, no one was able to gather much of importance, just small tidbits that were too vague to help – rough, foreign men had sailed in at the end of summer. Their captain went by the name Terrick, which didn't tell them anything. No one knew the Left-Handed's real identity. Terrick's crew had hung around for a few weeks, but they were gone now.

"Very interested in the black pearl business," a man remembered. "Wanted to know what powers the pearls had." He cackled. "As if pearls hold magic. Daft, that's what he was."

It wasn't until the fourth night on the island that Serb came back with information that sobered them all.

"Got to talking with the tavern owner tonight. I asked him about the pearl business, tried to hint at finding out who else was interested – you know, to gain advantage over our competitors. He mentioned Terrick's ship. He said the day after they sailed, his friend discovered that his warehouse had been raided. His pearls and sea gems had been stolen, replaced by similar-looking crates that were empty. So no one really knows when it actually happened. Of course, it was the end of the season, so most of his stock had already been shipped to the mainland of Kerrynth, but it was still a nasty blow. No way of knowing if it was Terrick or not, but they couldn't trace anything to anyone here."

"That would confirm their piracy, if we could be sure they did it, but we still don't know if they were even connected to the person we're looking for," Captain Markus reasoned.

"Although we have the prerogative to capture smugglers, don't we?" Petra spoke up.

The Captain nodded, but Serb broke in before he could speak. "That's not the end of it. A storm hit that night and by the afternoon of the second day, evidence of a shipwreck was washing up on shore. People struck out immediately to look for survivors, but other than three bodies and bits of wreckage, nothing was found. One of the bodies was Terrick's. The tavern owner said he saw him himself and he'd swear it was him, except that his left hand was missing. The nub was old, so it hadn't happened during the storm, but he had never noticed the man's missing hand when he was on land."

Everyone was silent as the story sunk in.

Terrick was either a victim of the assassin, or the assassin himself, and the story of him taking to piracy only fit that he was the latter.

If he was the Left-Handed, he was dead. Joran's brow furrowed as he considered it. He'd dreamed of killing the man himself for a while now, or at least the gratification of finding him and putting him in chains so he could pay for his crimes. He'd fantasized about tearing the story out of the man, to understand what had happened to Krynn and who had paid him for her death.

He waited for a kick to the gut. Those dreams would probably never come true. He'd never know for sure if his mother had paid an assassin to make Krynn disappear. Deep in his heart he felt it was the truth, but he'd never have proof. His mother had already died for her sins and now the Left-Handed himself had died, or so it seemed. Surely drowning wasn't an easy death, but it wasn't what Joran had wanted for him. He'd wanted the beast to know why he was dying, to face his sins and feel every moment of his death. It hurt to know that none of that could happen. Queen Lilian and the Left-Handed, and even Krynn, were all sealed in the past and there was no changing it. No joy of revenge, no peace in knowing the whole story. It hurt, but it didn't devastate him.

He'd spent a long time looking back.

He felt Petra's long fingers slide in between his and squeeze. Maybe he was finally ready to let the past stay there and begin walking into the future.

CHAPTER TWENTY-SEVEN

They had sailed around the Smyer Isles for a few more days, but hadn't found anything. Finally, Captain Markus set their course south to Kestell so they could get out of the Myah Sea before it grew dangerous with floating ice from the North Strait.

"We're heading home, men," the Captain boomed, smiling. The sailors moved with an eagerness in their steps. It had been six months since they'd first left port in Kestell. Some of the men had a family they were longing to see and others were just looking forward to the downtime in a familiar place. The Pearl would have her annual tar coat. The sails were due for oiling and Captain Markus had to report to the guard and receive the next half a year's salary for his crew.

***

The few weeks it took them to sail back went too quickly, and before he was ready, the voyage was over. They were there. Kestell.

The harbor looked almost the same, except that winter had dulled the colors. He remembered his first abrupt morning there. He remembered being hauled on board the Pearl, anger thrumming in his ears the whole time. The Captain's sternness. His pouches of jacin sinking beneath the water. The glory of the unending sea being the only thing that tempted his attention away from his miring.

Only a few months ago, but nothing was the same anymore. Not with him. He breathed in, the brine and fish scent familiar now, and he smiled.

He turned to Petra. She was leaving soon. Next month he would be back on the Pearl when she cast off, but Petra would be home in Cleft.

"I have an idea," he said nonchalantly, mischief dancing in his eyes.

Petra's black ones narrowed.

"I'll tell you when we disembark. But I'll need your rope drawing."

***

Joran had told her his idea, half expecting her to raise her fine eyebrow and say no, but she hadn't.

The tattooer worked in a small favela behind an ale house. It was the middle of the day, but unsavory people trickled around the area. The general squalor made his nerves hum with excitement. Petra walked easily beside him, composed and confident, easy even in the middle of this part of town.

The tattooer grunted at them when they entered.

"Can you do an interlocking knot?" Joran questioned, showing him the sketch.

He grunted again. "Who's first?"

Joran went first. When he was finished, he inspected the dark image on his bruised skin. The loose ends of the two separate ropes trailed off into nothingness, the bond where they met intricately detailed. The man was an artist. Joran's arm ached, but he flexed his muscles anyway, watching the ropes ripple, and grinned.

"Wait for me outside," Petra said.

He glanced at the stony man, then back at Petra. "Why?"

"Because I might scream and I don't want to be embarrassed. Go."

He knew she wouldn't scream. He went anyway, hovering near the door, uncomfortable about her being in there with the tattooer, even if she was dressed like a man. Joran knew she was Petra now and he could never unsee it. He couldn't figure out how he hadn't seen it before.

When Petra finally came out, she looked paler than usual, but her eyes were bright.

"Let me see?" Joran asked, his eyes searching her curiously.

She shook her head. "Not yet."

"What, really?" He pouted. "Yours is the same as mine, right? Wait – did you even do it?" He stopped short, spinning to face her.

She laughed. She didn't laugh often, but it was a clear, musical sound that made his heart stutter.

"You didn't!" He accused.

"I did. Truly. You just can't see it yet."

***

The next morning at breakfast, Petra winced as she joined him at the table. "You didn't tell me a tattoo would bruise this much," she accused.

He rolled his arm and shrugged. "Mine feels a lot better already."

She simply pursed her lips and took a seat.

She was annoying with her stubbornness. She still hadn't let him see the tattoo. He had come up with the idea that they imprint themselves with matching ink designs under their skin, a mark that wouldn't fade away. The interlocking knot design would symbolize how their lives had entwined together, never to part.

They'd promised each other their lives, but she wouldn't even let him see the tattoo? He tried to brush away his bruised feelings.

"Sad to see you go, Petra," Serb said.

She shifted. "Thanks, Serb. You all have been like family. I'll see you again, I know it."

She turned to Joran. "I have to catch Kirk to thank him for his cabin and meet with the Captain before I go."

He nodded before noticing how she was listing to the side while seated. Realization clicked, and he flushed, mostly with excitement.

His girl. His *spicy* girl. He loved her so much.

"You devil, Petra. I know why you won't let me see it," he said.

"Oh?" She feigned innocence.

"You did *not* put our pledge across your backside, did you?"

The crew's eyes shot to him. Then to her, and someone chuckled.

Joran swiped at his forehead, grinning at the men to play it off, although he hadn't meant for them to hear. "She keeps things interesting," he bragged with a wink.

Petra smirked slightly, rising with her empty bowl, and Joran almost tripped over his boots to follow her, ignoring the laughter of the men behind him.

Petra set her bowl down in the galley then turned to him. "I told you, you couldn't see it yet. Someday…" she said, coyly, and his stomach flipped. Fire rushed through his core and he grabbed her, wrapping his arms around her and pulling her close.

"Soon," she finished, the word a whisper in his ear.

He pressed his lips to hers, memorizing the feel of cool silk against his tongue, trying to implant every soft contour on his own lips so he would never forget. She parted her mouth in welcome, letting him explore, then taking the lead, she sucked hard on his bottom lip. The action sent sparks through him and he groaned softly.

His legs were going weak as he leaned in, pressing his body against hers. Her breasts were heavy against his chest, her heartbeat melding with his. For a few moments, time stopped and they breathed together, their hearts pumping against each other, living as one.

It was hard to tear himself away.

Her lips were pink and wet and he groaned, trying to keep himself from losing himself in them again.

He was sure the others had seen their affectionate display earlier and he hardly cared, but there were no bold eyes watching them now. He was grateful for their respect.

He contented himself with tracing the lines of her face, her cheekbones, her jaw, her chin, the feel of the soft wisps of hair that fell over her ears and down her neck.

"Write to me, *Peter*," he said. His eyes sparkled, but his voice was thick with desire. "Write to me every day. I'll see you in six months and then I'll never leave you again. I promise." He clapped his hand over his upper arm to indicate the knot tattoo.

Petra smiled. "You write to me too, even if it means you have to send a crate full of mail at every port. I'll be waiting for you when you return."

Joran would finish his year conscription with Captain Markus and then he would go home. He had already written to his father to tell him he wanted to return to help him rebuild his shaken kingdom. He wanted to be there for his family, for Benrid, his older brother and the crown prince, and for Golan, his younger brother who he barely knew. He even wanted to be there for King Henry. They had a lot of catching up to do to make up for lost time. And he wanted to be with Petra. Forever.

He pulled something out of his pocket and slipped it around her neck. The luminous black orb dangled from the end of a leather strap. It was depthless, but other colors formed a shimmery veil around it. Purple, silver, and blue hues flickered in the sunlight. It was unassuming, a plain jewel that blended in, but if you looked closely, was full of infinite beauty. Like Petra.

"Your pearl," she said simply, touching her fingers to the pearl he'd bought in Bristia.

"Yours," he corrected. "But you're mine." His smile was devastating.

***

Petra left less than an hour later. He escorted her to a coach which was departing that hour. They would make the next city by nightfall.

She climbed inside, then leaned back toward him. "I left you something on the ship," she said.

When he climbed back aboard the Pearl he took the stairs two at a time. Nestled in his swinging bed was a folded paper. "*Your first letter,*" was written on the outside, and he smiled, opening it slowly. The other side made his chest tight. She'd drawn a story, a lifetime, on one page. Behind him was a longbow, a river, and a bird. Behind her, a bird, a sword, and a crystal. Then they were together, taking up most of the page, holding on to each other, but gazing into the future. His new sword swung from his belt, his upper arm banded in black rope. She stood beside him in her black shirt and breeches, her hair tousled by the wind, her chin lifted courageously. He caressed her image on the page with his finger tip, sighing before refolding the paper and tucking it into his pocket. He'd find somewhere safe for it, but for now he wanted it close. The ship felt empty without her.

He strode out to the stern, which faced the open sea.

Captain Markus came up beside him.

"I'm proud of you, Joran. If you ever need somewhere to go after this year, my ship is always welcome," he said gruffly, before moving away.

Water stretched before Joran, caught up in its endless dance all the way to the horizon. He lingered at the rail to watch it, letting everything sink in. All the memories, all thoughts of the future, all the emotions. And all he felt was peace.

ACKNOWLEDGMENTS

My first thanks goes to my Heavenly Father, the One Who gave us the gift of language and gave me a love for it. He is the One Who is with me through the story of my own life and cares enough about me to listen when I come to Him in the middle of the night in angst about plot holes in my fantasy novel.

I also want to thank my parents, both of whom love to read. I learned from their example and by listening to stories on their laps from the time I was born. My mother taught me how to read, and my father was always ready to answer my "What does this word mean" and "How do you spell this" questions. They invested in books so I would always have quality reading material, and they encouraged my love for writing.

Thank you to Josh, my husband, who gave up many hours with me to allow me to be in front of my screen instead. He took the girls to work with him or put them to bed many times just so I could have a few more minutes to write. He has listened to me tell my tales, even though he doesn't care for fantasy, and he didn't blink an eye when I told him I wanted to publish. I would not be who I am today without his love and support.

Thank you to my daughters, Mercy and Selah, for being as excited about my book as I am. They asked endless questions about how the book would look and when it would be printed. They begged me to tell them "more of the story" before bed each night, and they've even named dolls after my characters. They are my cheer squad.

Thank you to all the authors who have written books. It is your stories I enjoyed, your stories that taught me to appreciate the written word and learn the art of storytelling. You are my biggest inspiration. You are my teachers. To those of you who are active on social media, thank you for being part of the wonderful reading and writing community out there, being candid about your struggles and mistakes, being real and letting the rest of us see that you are human too, and blessing us with your books.

Thank you, Joyce, at Rejoyce Literary Editing, for your time and dedication to this book. Your insight is all over these pages, and I am so glad, because *Of Oceans and Pearls* is so much better with it. You never failed to encourage me every single time we interacted, and I needed it! It kept me going.

My gratitude would not be complete without thanking you, bookish friend. It takes a lot of faith to venture into an indie publisher's first novel, and I am so grateful to you for taking that step for me. Thank you for choosing my book and making my dreams come true. Please follow me online or sign up for my newsletter so we can keep in touch, and please consider leaving me a review. Ratings and reviews make all the difference for authors like me – they are how we get seen in the big, wonderful book world. Thank you so much.

Bonus: If you leave a review online, you can send me a link to it, and I'll email you a link to bonus scenes from Petra's point of view.

Instagram:
https://www.instagram.com/reneeknightauthor/

TikTok:
https://www.tiktok.com/@reneeknightauthor

Pinterest:
https://www.pinterest.com/reneeknightauthor/

Milton Keynes UK
Ingram Content Group UK Ltd.
UKHW031443291124
451807UK00005B/390